PEPPERMINT
CREAM
DIE

PEPPERMINT CREAM DIE

THE HSP MYSTERIES

CAROL E. AYER

CAMEL
PRESS
Kenmore, WA

CAMEL PRESS

A Camel Press book published by Epicenter Press

Epicenter Press
6524 NE 181st St.
Suite 2
Kenmore, WA 98028

For more information go to:
www.Camelpress.com
www.Coffeetownpress.com
www.Epicenterpress.com
www.carolayer.com

This is a work of fiction. Names, characters, places, brands, media, and incidents are either the product of the author's imagination or are used fictitiously.

Cover and interior design by Scott Book and Melissa Vail Coffman

Peppermint Cream Die
Copyright © 2020 by Carol E. Ayer

ISBN: 978-160381-618-2 (Trade Paper)
ISBN: 978-160381-629-8 (eBook)

Library of Congress Control Number: 2020934862

Printed in the United States of America

To my grandmother, Isabel Ferguson.
I can only hope to be as vital and creative in my sunset years as you.

ACKNOWLEDGMENTS

I'D LIKE TO THANK MY AGENT, Dawn Dowdle, and my editor, Jennifer McCord, for their hard work and support. Dawn guided me in turning the nugget of an idea into an actual manuscript and Jennifer gave me immeasurable assistance in making this the best book it could be.

Many thanks to Elaine Aron for writing the definitive work about the HSP trait. I don't think it's hyperbole to say that *The Highly Sensitive Person* changed my life.

I found the book *Start a Cake Business: How to Succeed in a Home-Based Cottage Food Operation or a Commercial Kitchen* by Paula Spencer to be a huge help in figuring out the details of Kayla's job.

Thank you to my mom, Penny Strohl, and my bestie, Johan Steiner, for your endless love and encouragement.

Lastly, I want to recognize my fellow HSPs . . . may your life be at the exact level of stimulation that is just right for you. Never forget that the world needs your gentle nature.

CHAPTER 1

I WATCHED IN HORROR AS THE TOP tier slid slowly but surely off the rest of the cake and splattered onto the floor. The sponge crumbled into a million pieces and the frosting smeared its way across the room. The judges gasped. The other contestants gasped. I gasped.

"No!" I cried. I couldn't believe it. All that work wasted.

"You should go on one of those competitions," a voice said.

I shook myself out of my devastation and turned my attention from the TV to my friend Trudy Dillingham, who I'd completely forgotten was watching the show with me. She sat in my easy chair, eyeing me carefully.

"Oh, I couldn't," I said. "You forget that I'm an introvert."

"Yes, dear, and a highly sensitive person. You're also an extremely good baker and you could probably win one of those shows." Trudy folded up her knitting and placed it in her tote bag as scenes from next week's episode ran across the screen.

I exited from DVR mode, unfolded myself from my comfortable position on the microsuede couch, and stood to stretch. "But did you see how upset I was about someone else's cake? Someone I don't even know?"

Trudy adjusted her green silk scarf. The hue of the scarf almost exactly matched the color of her eyes and was a nice contrast to her short silver hair. "I like your sensitivity and compassion, but sometimes you need to break through your fears and do things you don't want to. You might end up having the best adventure of your life, or, at the least, an excellent learning experience."

"I'll think about it. Hey, I made you a peppermint cream pie to take to the senior center, an early holiday treat. Now that Halloween's over, the stores are bringing in their Christmas stuff and the candy canes were on sale."

Trudy rose from the easy chair with the agility more befitting a much younger woman. "You're a darling. Thank you. I better get moving. I want to give Sugar a few Meow Munchables before I go to the center."

I stepped through the small dining room into the kitchen to retrieve the pie from the refrigerator. I nestled it into a paper bag with handles and returned to the living room. "Give her a kiss for me."

"I will."

I saw Trudy to the door. Just before she left, she turned and pulled me into a hug, giving me a start. It was unusual for her to embrace me. She once said she wanted to be respectful of my personal space since I was sometimes sensitive to touch. I didn't always like being hugged, particularly when I felt overstimulated, but today I happily wrapped my arms around her petite frame.

After I closed the door, I returned to the kitchen to wash the dishes and cups Trudy and I had used during her visit. While I worked, I reflected on her suggestion of entering a TV baking competition. I'd have to make an audition video first, which made my heart race just thinking about. Assuming I made it onto the show, I'd be forced to contend with the sensory overload; bright lights, noise, bad feelings among the contestants, and, worst of all, judging. How could I possibly perform to the best of my ability with millions of people watching? I couldn't think of anything more stressful, and my entire existence was built on keeping stress at bay.

Three years earlier, burned out from a decade of working customer service in a chaotic environment and close to falling into a depression, I took advantage of my company's mental health program and sought help from the in-house counselor. She proposed that I might be an HSP, gave me a copy of Elaine Aron's *The Highly Sensitive Person*, and gently suggested I was in the wrong line of work.

I devoured the book and found myself in its pages. As an HSP, I was hypersensitive to sounds, smells, and other sensory stimuli, and easily became overwhelmed by the input. I picked up on other people's moods and felt my own emotions strongly. I took criticism to heart and had a hard time getting over negative experiences. On the plus side, I was creative, compassionate, and conscientious. I might have been good for my customer service job, but it wasn't good for me.

Meanwhile, I'd been thinking about moving. My apartment on the top floor of a nine-unit building was hot in the summer, close to a busy street, and blocks away from Adam, the boyfriend I'd recently broken up with. I yearned to be out of the city and near the water.

A complete life makeover was in order. My late grandmother had left me an inheritance which produced a nice bit of interest, so I had a cushion. I resigned from my job and brainstormed where to live.

I'd always enjoyed family trips to Oceanville on California's central coast. I searched on the web and found an in-law cottage for rent in Seaside Shores, a non-gated planned community built into a hillside overlooking Oceanville Bay. Clicking through to the community's website in search of more information, I found that Seaside Shores was home to young single professionals, families, and retirees. I filled out an online application, exchanged emails with the landlord, and a month later, packed up and left the San Francisco Bay Area, where I'd lived all my thirty-two years.

By the time I'd settled into the cottage, I had the germ of an idea for a new job. The counselor had told me many HSPs transition to self-employment in a way to control their work hours and environment. My mom had taught me how to bake, and we'd spent many a happy hour in the kitchen whipping up desserts. I'd found the activity soothing, creative, and fun, and I'd delighted in the heady scents of vanilla, cinnamon, and peppermint.

I did some research and discovered that California allowed home bakery businesses under its Cottage Food Law. Eight months later, I opened Kayla's Home-Baked Goods by the Sea.

Supplemented by the interest from my inheritance, my business allowed me to pay the rent, feed myself, and buy the baking supplies I needed. Because I wasn't allowed under the law to sell anything that required refrigeration, I specialized in non-perishable ocean-themed creations.

My cell rang as I was scrubbing the kitchen counters in preparation for work mode. I went back to the living room and rummaged around in the couch cushions until I came up with the phone.

Trudy was on the other end. "Kayla, dear, I'm here at the center and just found out bingo's starting early today. They're moving around times and rooms for some fancy schmancy private party. I'm going to stay straight through and not come home until later. Would you mind running over to give Sugar her wet food? Around three thirty?"

I checked the clock and saw it was now two thirty. "Sure. No problem. The key's in the fake rock in the garden?"

"Yes. Thank you. And thank you again for the pie."

"My pleasure. Enjoy."

I FINISHED CLEANING THE KITCHEN AND TURNED my attention to the birthday cake I'd made for Catherine Chiu. Catherine, or Cat as she was affectionately known, had founded Seaside Shores's popular book club. The day before, I'd constructed a stack of books made from chocolate cake covered in different-colored fondant. Now, I took my piping tips from the pantry and added classic sea-themed titles along the sides of the books using Cat's name: *Cat's Travels*, *Catherine Crusoe*, and *Moby Cat*.

I put the cake back under its dome, cleaned the kitchen again, and printed the invoice and required labels for the bakery box. I grabbed my messenger bag and left the house. Heading for the scenic coastal path that originated south of Seaside Shores, ran the length of the community, and ended at Oceanville Wharf, I strolled over my driveway and across a planked walkway to avoid getting sand in my shoes. Once I'd joined the coastal path and was walking north to Trudy's house, I breathed in the sea air, glanced out at the waves breaking toward the shore, and basked in the peacefulness of my community.

Contentment washed over me. I was living the perfect life for an HSP: peaceful, creative, and beautiful. I felt like the luckiest girl in the world.

Yes, it was the perfect life . . . until I arrived at Trudy's to find her lying in the foyer with her silk scarf wrapped much too tightly around her neck.

ONE OF THE RESPONDING OFFICERS ESCORTED me outside to the white bench Trudy had installed in her front garden the spring before. How I wished I could go back to the day when Trudy and I gave the bench a trial run. We'd gazed companionably out at the ocean, the sun caressing our faces on the cool day.

After the officer took my statement, he passed me off to a man dressed in a blue suit who introduced himself as Detective Kenneth Shapiro. He asked me many of the same questions the officer had, including when I'd seen Trudy last. I told him I'd spoken to her at two thirty and seen her an hour or so before that.

"Did you notice anything unusual, either when you saw her or spoke with her on the phone?"

I shook my head. "No. I can't think of anything."

"Did she seem tense or nervous?"

"Not at all." I wrapped my arms around myself. I'd been shivering nonstop since I found Trudy, partly from the chill in the fall air and partly from shock. "Wait, there is one odd thing. I don't know why she was home. She was supposed to be at the senior center playing bingo. It's why she had me come over to feed Sugar. Sugar is her cat." I had never even seen Sugar. I hoped she was all right.

"We'll talk to people at the senior center. Do you have any idea why she might have come home? Was she not feeling well?"

"I don't think so. She looked fine. I gave her a peppermint cream pie to take to the center. She was happy about it. When she found out bingo was starting earlier than usual today, she called and asked me to feed Sugar. Everything was normal."

"Had she asked you to feed Sugar before?"

"Oh sure. She often asked me to do it when she wasn't going to be home at three thirty. She was diligent about feeding Sugar at the same time each day." I was surprised I knew how to form coherent sentences. I felt like I'd been hit by a thousand cream pies all at once.

"Do you know of anyone she wasn't getting along with recently?"

I shook my head rapidly. "No. Absolutely not. Everyone loved her. She was a sweet elderly woman. You know, the grandmother type."

He looked down at the statement I'd provided to the police officer. "She didn't actually have children and grandchildren, though?"

"That's true. She never married. No kids or grandkids. Her last remaining relative, a sister, died a few months ago. The sister never married either. It was a small family."

"What about a caretaker or someone who came in to assist with chores?"

I shook my head.

After another fifteen minutes, the detective gave me the go-ahead to leave. I staggered away from what was now a bedlam of activity and headed back south on the coastal path in the direction of the community clubhouse. I needed my best friend, Isabella Valera.

As I walked, I remembered Trudy giving me the uncharacteristic embrace. Should I have told the detective? I debated calling him and decided against it. What was I going to say? Trudy had given me a suspicious hug?

Still, it led me to wonder. Did Trudy have a sixth sense she was about to die?

"I CAN'T BELIEVE THIS HAPPENED," I moaned to Isabella at the clubhouse restaurant, where she was the most popular waitress if also the one with the most attitude. Isabella wasn't the biggest believer in "the customer is always right." Although she had yet to turn thirty and stood barely five feet tall, she could be intimidating when she wanted to be. Don't get her started on anything to do with women's rights. She had a degree in women's studies from UC Oceanville and was saving money to go to law school.

Once I'd managed to stammer out what happened—my articulateness had left the building—Isabella had led me to a table overlooking the water, even bending my knees for me so I could sit.

"Hold that thought," she said now. "I'm gonna get you some coffee."

When she came back, I moaned some more about how unbelievable everything was.

She patted my hand. "I know. It's absolutely beyond comprehension. Here, drink this. It'll warm you up. Don't worry, it's decaf. I know how caffeine affects your sleep, especially this late in the day."

"I doubt I'll be sleeping much anyway."

She placed a steaming cup of black coffee in my hands, and I took a big gulp with no clue how hot it was and how bitter its taste. I managed to swallow, but I burned my mouth in the process.

"Poor, poor Trudy," I said. "She was eighty-nine. Who would do such a thing to an elderly woman? She must have been so frightened. I can't stand thinking about it."

Isabella slipped into the chair next to me. "It really is unimaginable. Oh, sweetie, you're still shivering. Take my sweater." She took off her white beaded sweater and draped it across my shoulders. It smelled deliciously of her gardenia perfume. "It's a good thing you agreed to feed Sugar. Who knows how long it would have taken for someone to find Trudy."

I'd taken another swallow of coffee and I gracelessly spurted it out onto the table. "Sugar. I forgot about Sugar. I have to feed her, give her water, play with her, clean her litterbox—"

"Kayla, I'm sure she's fine. You don't have to do all that right this second."

Unfazed by the mess I'd made, Isabella mopped it up with a napkin.

"But what am I going to do with her? With Sugar?"

"I'm sure a family member will take her in."

"That won't work. Remember? Trudy's sister was her last remaining relative. I guess I can ask her friends and neighbors, or maybe someone at the senior center wants a cat." I ran through the possibilities in my head as I fidgeted with my necklace. I could put a notice in the community newsletter or an ad in the Oceanville newspaper . . .

"Or . . ." Isabella rolled her hand around, apparently trying to get me to some conclusion she'd already reached.

"Or what?"

"Well, you have an obvious solution staring you in the face."

"I do? What?"

"You could take Sugar. You love cats. Didn't you tell me that HSPs often develop deep connections with animals?"

I shook my head a few times. "Yes, that's true. But I can't take care of a pet. It's hard enough taking care of myself."

"You're running a business. You keep yourself fed, and I've never seen you forget to put clothes on." She gave me a quick grin. "I think you're doing fine."

"Only because I've arranged my life just so."

"Exactly. How many people can say that? It's impressive."

"I guess."

"Let's be honest here. That's not the real reason, is it?"

"Of course it is. This coffee is awful, by the way. Could I have some milk? Or sugar? Or both? Maybe even an entirely different drink?"

"What was I thinking? It must be the shock over Trudy. I'm so sorry. I'll be right back."

While Isabella was away, I stared out the window at the ocean. I knew exactly what she was talking about. After a few inconsequential relationships in my twenties, at the age of thirty, I met a guy who was smart, funny, and handsome, everything I could have asked for. He'd been understanding about my introversion and sensitivity . . . until he wasn't. One day he blew up at me, annoyed I didn't want to go to a party, and that was that. We broke up. It had been a letdown, to put it mildly. Truth be told, I'd fallen hard for Adam and breaking up with him was one of the most traumatic events of my life. Now Trudy was gone. What if I let Sugar into my home, became attached to her, and lost her too?

Isabella returned. "Here's a decaf vanilla latte. Heavy on the syrup."
She sat again.

"Thanks, Iz."

"So, where were we? Oh yes. No matter what you say, I know you're having a hard time after Adam. You're afraid to let anyone close, even a pet."

"You know, I should get going. I have to start a wedding cake tonight. Just because I've had a horrendous experience doesn't mean I can ruin a bride's special day. I'll take the coffee with me. Can you bring my check and a to-go cup?"

"You're changing the subject."

"Iz, this is overwhelming for me, okay? My friend was . . . murdered." A shudder ran through me. Was this for real? I was now a person who knew people who were murdered? "Can we put off the Sugar conversation until later? I need to bake right now."

"Sure, hon. The coffee's on me." She got up to grab a to-go cup.

I poured the coffee in. "Thanks."

"I'll see you later. Good luck with the cake."

I DIDN'T HAVE A WEDDING CAKE TO make. I felt badly for lying to Isabella, but I couldn't take the conversation anymore. Instead of going home, I headed to the beach below the clubhouse and regarded the ocean, aware more than ever of the dangerous dark side to its great beauty.

I sat, scooped up a handful of sand, and let it run through my fingers, thinking about Trudy. We'd met three weeks after I moved to Seaside Shores. On Election Day, I lost my way coming home from the community offices, where I'd cast my ballot. Trudy, who was walking home from doing the same, guided me back to my cottage, even though it was in the opposite direction of where she was headed. I invited her in for cookies, and we had dinner two nights later. Gradually, we became friends.

When I confided in Trudy that all my grandparents had died, she took on the role of substitute grandmother with gusto. She knitted blankets for my bed. She bragged about my baking to everyone she knew. Best of all, she was always there to talk to when I was flipping out from stress or noise. I remembered the day I'd run to her when a jackhammer was about to drive me insane. She'd known exactly what to do. She settled me in a comfy chair, brought me a cup of tea, and put low, soothing music on her old stereo.

Tears streamed down my face. But the tears were swiftly followed by a great swell of anger. Someone had coldly and deliberately strangled one of the dearest friends I'd ever had.

Who did it and why?

CHAPTER 2

I USED THE BOTTOM OF MY SHIRT to clean my tear-stained glasses and finger-combed my wavy shoulder-length blond hair. Isabella's sweater was still draped over my shoulders. I put it on and inhaled the scent of gardenias. Then, beset by a strange combination of grief, restlessness, and exhaustion, I decided to do something I didn't normally do.

I didn't like going to restaurants alone; I always felt too self-conscious. The only exception I made was the clubhouse restaurant, and only during one of Isabella's shifts. But I had a hankering for clam chowder I didn't think I could shake. I rejoined the coastal path and took it all the way to Oceanville Wharf.

Not minding the hustle and bustle for once, I navigated my way through the tourists as they explored shops, laughed at sea lions bellowing on the rocks below, read restaurant menus, and accepted sample cups of chowder. The crowd and noise kept me from remembering the sight of Trudy's body and thinking about her last moments.

I walked to the end of the wharf and entered a restaurant I'd never been to, called Fishes Do Come True. The hostess led me to a small table near the kitchen and handed me a menu. No more than ten minutes later, I was seeking refuge in the warm creaminess of a large bowl of chowder. I dipped sourdough bread into the soup and ate with abandon. Both the chowder and the bread were delicious and exactly what I needed.

Halfway through my dinner, I noticed a dark-haired man with eyes as blue as the nearby ocean smoothly traveling from table to table, checking on the diners. He chatted with an older couple, who I pegged as married.

The husband said something that made the man throw his head back and laugh in delight. The man shook the husband's hand, leaned down to kiss the wife's cheek, and came over to me. He looked to be about my age.

"How are you enjoying your chowder?" he asked.

"It's fantastic," I said. "And the bread is out of this world."

"Thanks. I make them both. I'm the owner and manager, but I do some of the cooking too."

"No kidding. I'm a baker, myself. I run a business out of my home called Kayla's Home-Baked Goods by the Sea. Everything has an ocean-themed touch."

"That's very interesting, and coincidental. I've been thinking about changing up our desserts. Do you have a card?"

"Sure." I pulled one from my messenger bag and handed it to him.

He read the card. "Kayla Jeffries. Nice to meet you, Kayla. I'm Jason Banks." He offered his hand and I accepted the shake.

"Likewise," I said. "This is such a neat restaurant. I like the nautical décor. Some of the restaurants go overboard, so to speak, but I think you've done it just right."

"Thank you. So, how about doing me a favor? I've been getting desserts from a bakery in town and could use some feedback from a pro. Will you try a piece of cake on the house and let me know what you think?"

I grinned. A rough job but somebody had to do it. "I'd be happy to."

He brought me a slice of chocolate cake, which I tucked in to after I'd polished off the rest of my chowder and every piece of bread from the basket. It was okay, but, at the risk of sounding cocky, not as good as mine. I told Jason so, as tactfully as I could, when he came back for my verdict.

"I'll bring you one of my chocolate cakes," I said. "Complimentary. Then you can decide if you want to order from me."

"Deal. I've gotta get going. More chowder to make."

"Of course. Nice to meet you. I'll bring you the cake in a day or two."

Jason went through the door to the kitchen. The waitress came with my check, and I paid and left a tip.

Deciding to take the long way home, I walked down the wharf, glancing in a few stores on the way, and passed through the parking lot. On Wharf Road, I crossed Marine Parkway to access the formal entrance to Seaside Shores. Once I'd reached the welcome sign, I was guided by the moonlight and not much else. I'd read on the community website that the designers had believed too many lights would interfere with the surrounding nature—ironic, since I couldn't see much of anything at the moment. A light fog had moved in, making the visibility worse.

A touch of apprehension settled in my stomach. Trudy had been murdered not that many hours ago. Fortunately, it wasn't that late in the evening and cars passed by me on a regular basis. I told myself I was fine.

To stave off more thoughts of the murder, I reviewed my evening. I ate alone at a restaurant *and* managed to nab a potential new client. Trudy would have been so pleased. The fact that I couldn't tell her brought back the sense of loss that threatened to bring me to my knees. I couldn't fathom how someone could hurt her, let alone murder her. If I hadn't found her myself, I wouldn't have believed it.

I spent a restless night dreaming about shadowy figures entering my bedroom to strangle me. In one dream, a masked intruder broke into Trudy's house as I watched, grabbed her by her emerald green scarf, and pulled as tightly as they could. I watched the murder happen and was helpless to stop it. When I woke, heart pounding and sweat dampening my forehead, I decided my subconscious was sending me a message: I had to do something. Her killer had to be caught.

ISABELLA HAD RECENTLY BEGUN DATING a detective from the Oceanville Police Department, so I had an inside source. She met Brian Fforde most days for breakfast before they went to work, so I called and asked her to find out if there had been any developments. She agreed to do what she could.

"Do you have any news?" I asked her a few hours later when I came down to the clubhouse restaurant for lunch. She'd brought me a dish of pasta with pesto sauce, the day's special.

"A little," she said, sitting in the chair next to me. "He and his partner, Lisa, have taken over the case. He was reluctant to talk about it too much because it's an active investigation, but I managed to wangle some information from him. He can't resist my smile."

I nodded. She did have a great smile. Not to mention a perfect figure, huge brown eyes with naturally long lashes that didn't require mascara, and an abundance of dark curls that threatened to spill out of her work ponytail.

"And?" I asked.

"Well, first of all, they don't consider you a suspect."

"*What*? I didn't even know that was a possibility."

Isabella shrugged.

As I recovered from the shock of Isabella's statement, I asked if the detectives actually had any suspects.

"No. But it hasn't been that long."

"Well, what are they doing about it? They should be working around the clock."

"Talking to people at the senior center. Her neighbors. So far they don't have much to go on. They don't have suspects *or* a motive."

"That doesn't sound very promising. I owe it to Trudy to make sure the monster is put away for good. I'm gonna see what I can find out myself." I sat up straighter, hoping to back up my words with my attitude.

"That sounds dangerous," Isabella said, a doubtful look on her face. "What if you get too close to the killer? And are you forgetting who you are? An introverted HSP?"

"I know. It sounds like a lot of stress. Way too much stress. But I can't sit back and hope the police find the person. I have to do something." I remembered my dream. No way was I letting this go.

Isabella's boss, Vincent, gave her the stink-eye from across the room.

"I better get back to work," she said.

"I'm gonna head home, then. Can I get this to go?"

"Sure, sweetie."

She brought me a box and I paid the check.

I'd promised Jason from Fishes Do Come True I'd bring him a cake. After finishing my lunch, I set to work, baking a chocolate cake and decorating it with chocolate seahorses I'd made from a mold. I packaged the cake in one of my light-blue boxes, affixed my conch shell logo sticker and required labels, and walked to the wharf. Jason was busy in the kitchen, so I left the cake with the hostess, saying I'd follow up later.

I'd been home half an hour when Cat Chiu's sister, Theresa, came by to pick up the book birthday cake. Theresa oohed and aahed and said nice things about my design. What was even nicer was the bonus she added to my check before taking off for Cat's party.

I'd just logged the payment in my software program when my cell phone rang. The caller identified herself as Trudy's neighbor, Eileen Nichols.

"Trudy told me you would take Sugar if anything ever happened to her," Eileen said after we'd commiserated over our shared loss.

"She did?" I went into the living room and collapsed onto the couch.

I'd been trying to ignore the Sugar problem. Was the issue going to be decided for me?

"She knew how much you loved her."

"Yes, that's true, but—"

"So . . ."

"I don't know about this. I'm awfully busy with my baking business, and . . . and other things." I reviewed the cottage food industry rules in my head. I was allowed to have pets, as long as they didn't enter the kitchen while I was creating products to sell. Although I never used it, a pocket door divided my kitchen from the dining room. I could easily keep the kitchen closed off from Sugar, so my business wouldn't work as an excuse. "Is there any chance you could take her?" I asked Eileen.

"I'm afraid not. I took her in last night, but I've been sneezing and coughing like crazy. I must be terribly allergic to her. It's not good for my asthma. Please, can you come get her and her things? I'm in the light-green house with the white trim next to Trudy's."

I struggled with the answer, but I didn't seem to have a choice. "Yes. Okay. I'll come right now."

I punched a bunch of holes in a cardboard box that once held a mixer and headed over to Eileen's in my mini-van. I averted my eyes from Trudy's house next door but managed to catch a glimpse of an alarming amount of crime scene tape.

Sugar wound herself around my legs in Eileen's living room. Eileen, a statuesque brunette in her early sixties, put a tissue to her nose.

"When did Trudy tell you about Sugar?" I asked her. "That I would take her, I mean."

"Not that long ago. In fact, I think it was the day before she died."

"What was the context?"

"She and Sugar were in the front garden and I came out for a chat. We commented on Sugar rolling around on her back in the sun, and how as a white cat, she could get sunburned. Trudy said she wanted Sugar to have a good home when she was gone. She told me you would take her."

"Okay." I picked up Sugar and placed her in the cardboard box, and Eileen helped me bring the cat's things to the mini-van. I waved good-bye to Eileen and went home with my new roommate.

After letting Sugar out of her box and setting up all her accoutrements— litter box in the spare room, bowls of food and water in the dining room, and toys in the living room—I eyed her warily, closed the pocket door to the kitchen so she couldn't go in, and left the house. I wasn't convinced taking in a cat was the best idea and I needed to clear my head.

I went for a walk along the beach, but hadn't gotten very far when I remembered that Sugar had just lost her caretaker. She'd been living next door in an unfamiliar place, and now she'd been left alone at a third house. My heart ached for her. I hurried back home, unlocked the front door, and rushed inside.

"Sugar, I'm back. I'm so sorry I left you."

She didn't come running. She wasn't where I'd last seen her, on the living room floor. She wasn't on the couch or in the easy chair. I went into the bedroom, but she wasn't there either. Nor was she in my office, the spare room, or the bathroom. This was just great. I'd had her for about five minutes, and I'd lost her already. I looked under the couch. No dice. I went back into the bedroom and found her curled up in a corner under the bed.

I said gently, "Sugar, it's okay to come out. I'll be honest with you, I'm a little scared. Both about having you as a roommate and trying to figure out who did that awful thing to Trudy yesterday."

She meowed plaintively.

"I'll be here if you decide to come out. I have plenty of food and an endless supply of water. All your toys are here too. You can't go into the kitchen, but otherwise, anything goes. It's a quiet place. I made sure of that."

The business phone rang from my office.

"Okay, so sometimes the phone rings. Hopefully you're okay with that noise."

I went into the office and looked at the caller ID. It read FISHES DO COME TRUE without a caller's name, so I answered with my professional spiel.

"Kayla's Home-Baked Goods by the Sea. Kayla speaking. How may I help you?"

"Hi, Kayla. This is Jason from Fishes Do Come True. I love the cake you brought. I'd like to place an order."

"Terrific."

I pulled up an order form on the computer. Jason asked for three chocolate cakes, and I quoted him a price, saying I'd get the desserts to him the next morning. Our business was complete, but he stayed on the phone.

"Is there anything else?" I asked.

"Yes. But this is personal, not business. I wondered if you'd like to go see a movie. If you're available."

"A movie?"

"Yeah. At first they were silent and then talking was added in the nineteen twenties. The first talkie was *The Jazz Singer*. They're shown on this great big screen in a place called a theater . . ."

I laughed uncertainly. "Right. I think I've seen one once or twice. Um, sure. Why not?"

"Tomorrow night? We could grab a drink and dinner beforehand at Sam's if that sounds good. Would six thirty work?"

"Okay. That sounds fine. I'll meet you there."

"Great. Looking forward. Bye, Kayla."

We hung up. I shuffled into the living room, sank into the couch, and stared at the soothing blue walls. What in the world was I doing? First Sugar and now Jason?

I reminded myself that sometimes change was good. I decided to ride the wave of putting myself out there and begin my investigation of Trudy's murder. I had an idea of where to start. Trudy came home early from playing bingo on the day she died. Perhaps someone who played alongside her knew why she'd left abruptly. I returned to the bedroom, saw that Sugar was now sleeping peacefully on top of the comforter, and set out on foot for the senior center, a short distance from Trudy's house.

As soon as I entered the building, I heard numbers being called from inside a room adjacent to the door. I went in. A woman with red hair pulled back into a bun greeted me from a long table covered with stacks of bingo cards.

She said, "They'll be starting a new game soon. Each card is a dollar."

"Okay. Sure, I'll take one." I took my wallet from my messenger bag and handed her a single.

I joined a table of six people, but no one took notice of me. Everyone was too interested in the numbers being called. The caller, a woman with long, curly white hair, stood in the center of the room and removed balls one by one from a cage. The current game ended and a man verified his win. A new game began a few minutes later.

"I twenty-one, N forty," the caller chanted. "I nineteen."

Although I daubed four numbers in a row and only needed O 72 for a bingo, I didn't win. Neither did the diminutive elderly gentleman next to me, and he took it a lot harder than I did. He let loose a couple of obscenities and threw his bingo card onto the floor before stomping out of the room—an extreme reaction to a bingo game, I felt. Could he have this kind of reaction to other things, like to fellow player Trudy Dillingham?

I rushed out of the room. My bingo neighbor had left the building and was now on the coastal path, staring out at the water.

Waves gently rolled toward the shore under a perfectly blue sky. On the beach, a child picked up a strand of seaweed and wrapped it around her arm, delighted by her find. Near the water's edge, a sandpiper hurried along on its long legs. I couldn't believe I was about to talk about murder in such a peaceful setting.

"Hi," I said.

The man turned around. "What? Who are you? What do you want?"

"I'm Kayla Jeffries. I was inside at bingo. I just lost my first game and noticed you were kind of upset about not winning too."

"The whole thing's rigged. I don't know why I keep trying. Lost four games in a row."

"Is it that big a deal?"

"Yes, it's a big deal. Those bingo games can make someone a few hundred dollars at a time, Missie."

"Wow. Really?"

"Yes, really, and on a fixed income, it can mean a lot."

"I see what you mean, Mr . . .?"

"Engel. Burton Engel."

"Nice to meet you." He grunted in response and didn't react when I extended my hand to shake.

His lack of friendliness was almost enough for me to give up and go home. I remembered my reasons for being there and plowed ahead. "Did you know Trudy Dillingham, by any chance?"

"Unfortunately, I did," he said. He noticed my surprised reaction and made a gesture of apology. "Sorry, sorry. Friend of yours?"

"Yes. She was a very good friend to me. I'm also the person who found her and I'm trying to figure out who would have wanted to hurt her. Any ideas?"

"Me, for one."

CHAPTER 3

I STAMMERED, "YOU'RE NOT SAYING YOU KILLED HER, are you?"

"Did I say that? Of course not. But I was mad at her, that's for sure. She cheated at bingo. She was always winning and taking everyone's money."

"She never mentioned to me she'd made money playing bingo."

"I guess she wanted to keep it on the down-low, as my grandkids say. Maybe she was afraid of being robbed. Which is probably what happened. She was killed because she walked into the middle of it."

It was difficult to believe Trudy wouldn't have told me about the bingo money, nor did I understand how it was possible to cheat, but I nodded.

Burton didn't hesitate to chatter on. "Now that she's gone, I thought I'd have a chance. Nope. It's still rigged. Haven't won a single game. Now, if you'll excuse me, dinner is about to be served."

"Wait, before you go. Do you know why Trudy left the center earlier than expected yesterday? She was killed sometime between two thirty and three thirty."

"I have no idea. I lost every round is all I know. By the way, if you get any more half-baked ideas about me killing her, you can verify my whereabouts. I went straight from backgammon to the bingo room, and I was there from the beginning to the bitter end. I'm leaving now. I plan to drown my sorrows in macaroni and cheese."

I believed Burton and didn't feel it necessary to check his alibi immediately, but I made a mental note to do so if I needed to later. Planning to drown my own sorrows by ordering the biggest sandwich on the menu, I left for the clubhouse restaurant.

ISABELLA WAS BUSY WITH THE DINNER RUSH. She finally came over to take my order.

"I'll have a club sandwich with extra mayo and a side of fries," I said. "Iz, did Brian say anything about Trudy being robbed?"

"No, he said it wasn't a burglary."

"This guy at the senior center said she'd made a lot of money from bingo."

"I wouldn't know about that, but you might want to run it past Brian. Sorry, I have to keep moving. I'll bring your sandwich in a bit, sweetie."

One of Isabella's quirks was her propensity to call me "hon" and "sweetie" even though I was more than five years older. She brought over my dinner about fifteen minutes later. While I munched on my sandwich, I watched her interact with the other customers, admiring her confidence. She flirted and scolded, commiserated and encouraged. She was such an extrovert, but that was likely what made our relationship work. We were opposites. I appreciated her outgoing nature and she liked my quiet disposition. When I left a while later, I waved good-bye, grateful we were friends, and went home to fulfill Jason's order of chocolate cakes.

SATURDAY MORNING, I ATTACHED MY MAGNETIC business signs to each side of my mini-van and headed to the delivery parking lot at the wharf. I unloaded the three chocolate cakes to take to Fishes Do Come True. When I found out Jason wasn't there, I dropped off the desserts with the hostess, and half-disappointed and half-relieved, returned to my car.

I removed the magnetic signs and drove north to the police station in downtown Oceanville. The policewoman at the desk agreed to get Brian for me. She came back a few minutes later with a freckled, red-haired man who looked to be in his late thirties. After introducing myself as the person who'd found Trudy—and Isabella's best friend, for good measure—I brought up the bingo money.

Brian ran a hand through his curly hair. "I'm not supposed to be talking about this, but that fits. We found a lot of cash."

"It wasn't a burglary, for sure?"

"The money wasn't especially well-hidden. Just in her top dresser drawer. If the guy was looking for money, it was there for the taking. Her TV wasn't stolen, and her jewelry box was open but unemptied."

"How did the killer get inside?" The key had been under the fake rock as usual. I didn't remember seeing any indications of a break-in when I found Trudy lying in the foyer.

"There was no sign of forced entry. She opened the door for him—or her. Could have been a woman."

"Do you have any leads you can tell me about?" I asked.

Instead of answering, he said, "If you think of anything you haven't already told us, give me a call." He handed over a business card and we said good-bye.

THAT AFTERNOON, AS THE TIME OF MY DATE with Jason grew closer, a mix of excitement and nerves got my stomach churning. Even pleasant experiences sometimes overwhelmed me, and I wasn't entirely sure first dates qualified as such. It was at times like these I wished I were part of the thirty percent of HSPs who identified as extroverts rather than introverts. I had a powerful urge to stay home and read a book.

As I scoured my closet for something to wear, and debated whether to go at all, Sugar rubbed against my legs. She had made leaps and bounds—sometimes literally—in her confidence level. She now went through the house without fear, jumped on furniture, scratched the couch, and followed me around.

While I was deliberating and halfheartedly holding up shirts to myself, Sugar leapt onto the bed. She meowed at a short-sleeved top with an empire waist.

Taking that as her approval, I put it on, along with my nicest jeans and a red sweater. I pondered whether to wear my boots with the two-inch heel. I wasn't much taller than Isabella and sometimes liked to add a little height to my five-foot-two frame. Jason was probably six feet, so there was no chance of my towering over him, heels or not. I decided on ballet flats since I'd be walking to the wharf. After slipping them on, I went into the bathroom to apply lipstick and mascara. Before I could chicken out, I left the house.

I walked along the coastal path toward the wharf, taking deep breaths and gazing out at the water. The usual power of the ocean worked its magic, making me calmer almost immediately. Stopping for a moment, I watched an otter glide across the water on his back. Gorgeous oranges and reds blazed across the sky as the sun began to set, bringing tears to my eyes.

By the time I reached Sam's, I was feeling pretty good. But the noise inside the restaurant was earsplitting as tourists and locals celebrated

Saturday night. Jason came up to me and guided me to a table at the window, where the noise was even worse.

I tried to adjust. "Good to see you."

"What did you say?"

"Good to see you," I said, louder.

"It's noisy in here."

"Very."

"You don't look at all comfortable. I'll see if we can get a table outside. It will be quieter out there. They have heaters, so we shouldn't get cold."

Within minutes, we were settled outside at a table on the deck and each had a drink. It was mercifully quiet, and with a heater right next to our table, the perfect temperature. String lights and lamps gave the space an intimate feel.

I thanked Jason. "I have a thing about noise. A big thing, really. Like I absolutely can't stand it." I bowed my head, hoping he wouldn't think poorly of me. Although I'd fully accepted that I was an HSP, I often felt shy about sharing the trait's drawbacks with other people. I feared they'd conclude I was overreacting to something that didn't bother them as much, if at all.

"HSP?" Jason asked.

I looked at him in surprise. "You know what that is?"

"Yeah. My sister, Paula, is an HSP. I know how hard noise is. Whenever we went to Disney World as kids, she couldn't stand the fireworks. My mom had to take her back to the hotel while my dad and I stayed to watch. Certain fabrics bother her too. I think she tries a different kind of sheet every week."

I immediately relaxed. Although several books had been published about HSPs and a documentary made, I didn't often meet people familiar with the trait. It felt good to be around someone who understood my sensitivity from the outset.

Jason lifted his arms over his head and stretched. "Tell me more about yourself. Where do you live?"

"Seaside Shores, the planned community south of here."

"I know it. It's where my sister lives. The two of you should get in touch."

"And have an HSP party?" I laughed.

"Sorry. That's a dumb thing to say. Just because you share the same personality trait doesn't mean you'd hit it off."

"No, it's fine. I *would* like to meet her. I can see why she lives in Seaside Shores. It's peaceful. Quiet. That's why I live there. Well, it *was* peaceful, anyway. Until recent events."

"The murder on Thursday?"

"Yes. I'm actually the one who found Trudy."

Surprise passed over his face. "I'm sorry. Paula told me what happened, and I read about it in the paper, but I had no idea who found her."

I nodded, glad my name hadn't made it into the media.

"I can't imagine why someone would kill an elderly woman," Jason said. "I guess she must have interrupted a burglary."

"My friend's boyfriend is with the police, and he said nothing was taken. They think that she let the person in. There was no sign of forced entry."

"How odd."

"We were close. She was like a grandmother figure to me." A few tears made their way down my cheeks. "Excuse me." I rose to go to the restroom.

Jason put his hand on my arm. "Don't go on my account. You lost someone close to you. It's natural to cry. I don't know why we make it so socially unacceptable to show our feelings."

I returned to my chair. "That's nice of you." I took a tissue from my messenger bag, removed my glasses, and wiped my eyes.

"Hey, I cry at the drop of a hat," Jason said. "One of those guys who bawls at commercials, Christmas movies, and pet stories. Last week I cried watching the sun rise."

"Maybe you're an HSP too?"

"Could be. I'm not thrilled with leaf blowers, I can tell you that. If a busboy drops plates, I have to keep myself from blowing a gasket. Honestly, I wasn't too happy about those fireworks at Disney World, but I didn't want my dad to think I was a wimp."

"Leaf blowers are the worst."

"Have you ever had the unfortunate luck of being nearby when someone was power washing a building?"

"Yes. A few years ago before I moved here. The apartment building next to me was getting a power wash, and I had to leave the premises. That *is* the worst."

We laughed. I was having a good time. Near the end of my relationship with Adam, he said hurtful things like "grow up," "you need a thicker skin," and "stop being a hothouse flower." Here was someone who not only understood my sensitivity but might be in the same boat.

Our meals—salmon for Jason and scallops for me—arrived shortly. We chatted about books and movies as we ate. After we shared a piece of first-rate apple pie I could only hope to emulate, we walked down the wharf to Jason's Honda Civic to drive to the movie.

At the theater, I was pleased to find that the seats were cushy and could be adjusted like an easy chair. Jason joked that the seats were so comfortable and he was so stuffed from dinner that he might fall asleep. Despite our full stomachs, we shared a tub of popcorn while laughing throughout the movie.

JASON TOOK ME HOME, and I thanked him for a nice evening. He waited until I was safely inside before driving off.

Just as I was about to go in search of Sugar, someone knocked at the door. Had Jason come back? I looked through the peephole to see my landlord, Tristan Lawrence, illuminated by the outdoor light.

Tristan lived in a two-story home at the street, while I rented the in-law cottage down the driveway. Additional dwelling units had been approved by the community's board of directors six years earlier. Tristan had his aging mother in mind when he commissioned the construction of the five-room cottage, but by the time it was complete, Mrs. Lawrence had moved north to Oregon with a new beau. Tristan decided to rent out the addition, and I was lucky enough to be the chosen applicant once the original tenant moved on.

I opened the door and said hello.

With his roly-poly physique and greying mustache and beard, fifty-five-year-old Tristan fit right in when he dressed as a Santa Claus at Seaside Shores's annual holiday costume party.

"Kayla. I've been waiting for you to get home. You have to come see my new art." His brown eyes twinkled behind his trendy blue-framed glasses.

My heart sank. It was hard to express appreciation for artwork I didn't like. I rarely enjoyed Tristan's creations, but I always did my best to compliment him. I owed him. Not only had he accepted my rental application without ever laying eyes on me, he'd been instrumental in helping me get my business off the ground.

Although it was nearing eleven, I agreed. Stifling a yawn, I followed him to his back door. Thankfully, all his outdoor lights were on, so we could make our way there without stumbling on the uneven driveway.

Inside Tristan's house, I looked around. While his artwork bordered on the eccentric, his interior decorating was much like mine—soothing colors and comfortable furniture.

Tristan directed me to his studio, which he'd set up in a room near the front door. He pointed to the new work. A crab skeleton in a mound of sand and a canvas filled with gaping fish mouths greeted me.

"Oh. Well, wow." It was all I could come up with.

"I know, right? And guess what? I'm showing them with a few other pieces at the new gallery in town. The opening's next month on the twenty-first. SeaBlue Gallery. You'll come?"

"Sure. You know I won't be able to stay long."

"Right. I know. You and parties. Bring your new boyfriend, at least. I want as many of my peeps there as possible."

"My new boyfriend?"

"I can tell from a mile away that you have been on a date. You can't put anything past Uncle Tristan."

"I did have a date, yes. But he is not my boyfriend."

"The opening is *weeks* away. By then, you'll probably be inseparable."

I laughed. "You're very optimistic. It was only one date. Look, I've gotta go. I need to get some sleep. I have a birthday party tomorrow and I'm making the cake beforehand." I needed lots of rest time and deep sleep, especially after a particularly busy day. A visit to the police station and a date with a new guy were definitely in the category of maximum input.

"What kind of cake?"

"It's a beach-themed kids' party, so my octopus cake. Vanilla frosting tinged orange over yellow cake. I'll make the tentacles from gummy worms."

"Oooh. I'm sure it'll be wonderful. Will you show it to me on the way? And bring me a piece after if there's any left?"

"Of course." Tristan always liked my cakes, regardless of the kind or design. "See you in the morning."

I FELL ASLEEP QUICKLY. I woke briefly an hour or so later when a furry object jumped onto the bed and came up to the pillow. I scratched Sugar's chin and ears, reveling in the softness of her fur, and she settled in the crook of my body. She didn't move, nor did I, until six thirty the next morning. I'd remembered to set my clock back an hour when

I went to bed for the end of daylight saving time, so I'd gotten a good eight hours of sleep.

As I made up the batter for the yellow cake part of my octopus, I thought back on my date. I'd enjoyed myself and wouldn't mind seeing Jason again. Would he call? Isabella would say there was nothing wrong with me calling him but I didn't think I had the nerve.

While the cake rounds baked, I prepared the vanilla frosting and used red and yellow gel food coloring to tint it orange. Once the layers were cool, I laid one on top of the other and frosted them to make the octopus body. I added candy eyes and formed a smile from a gummy worm. Lastly, I attached stretched-out gummy worms all around the cake to make the tentacles. The finished product did look like an octopus.

I packed up the cake in my widest bakery box to accommodate the tentacles, changed into a blouse and black corduroys, and went out the front door. The sun was low and bright, a combination too arousing for me. I clipped on my sunglasses.

Before announcing myself at Tristan's back door, I admired the home's navy-blue exterior with turquoise trim. All the buildings in Seaside Shores were painted in colors that reflected the sea: different shades of blues and greens with touches of white. My cottage was painted a pretty teal.

Tristan answered immediately, his hands cupped around a coffee mug that read "ARTIST EXTRAORDINAIRE." I flipped open the top of the blue box and showed him the cake.

"Adorable," he said. "Where's the party?"

"Here in the community. The corner of Otter Street and Shell Lane."

"It's perfect. I know the kids'll love it."

"Thanks. I hope so. See you later."

"Don't forget to bring me a piece if you can," he called after me.

I joined the coastal path, breathing in the scents of seaweed and salt air. I adjusted my clip-ons and gazed out at the horizon. How I loved living in such a beautiful place. A pang shot through me when I remembered how much Trudy had loved Seaside Shores too. I trudged along, not noticing the beauty anymore.

I managed to get myself together by the time I arrived at the Fergusons'. A number of kids batted around a multi-colored beach ball in the front yard, while others jumped on an outdoor trampoline. I recognized one of Trudy's neighbors, Jan Williams, standing with some other parents near a picnic table decorated with ocean-themed paper goods and a scattering of seashells. We waved to each other.

I decided to stay so I could ask Jan about Trudy. I went through the front door to the kitchen and greeted the birthday mom, who was preparing sandwiches in the shape of starfish. At her request, I placed my boxed cake on the counter. She told me to help myself to a drink.

Outside again, I grabbed a root beer from the picnic table. Jan had separated from the other adults and was now watching the kids do tricks on the trampoline. I went over.

A gangly boy wearing goggles over his glasses performed a back flip and Jan called out her congratulations.

"Hey, Jan," I said. "Is that your son?"

"Kayla, how nice to see you. It's been a while. Yes, that's my Stewart. On his way to joining Cirque du Soleil. Did you make the cake?"

"Yep."

"Oh good. I'm glad I decided to stay."

"Thanks. Say, you heard about Trudy, I'm sure? I'm the one who found her."

Her eyes grew wide with horror. "You did? How terribly awful. To tell you the truth, we and the neighbors around us have been bundles of nerves ever since. What if it's some kind of serial killer? I heard nothing was taken. It wasn't a burglary."

That news had spread fast.

"I certainly hope it's not a serial killer," I said. "Do you have any thoughts about why someone would hurt Trudy, though? Was anyone mad at her, do you know?"

"I have no idea." Jan turned away and looked back to the trampoline. She clapped her hands when Stewart did a front flip.

One of my strengths was sensing when other people weren't comfortable. One minute, Jan was talkative, the next moment she wasn't. I was pretty sure she had just lied to me.

"You don't know of anyone who was upset with her?" I pressed.

She turned back. "Okay, listen. My husband and she had a little bit of a tussle. It was nothing, really. We've already spoken to the police about it."

"What happened?"

"Our dog had been barking in the evenings, maybe because Trudy had been having someone over. She came to the house one afternoon to complain, and she and Austin mixed it up a little. It wasn't the first time we'd had differences with her. She was a tough one."

I wouldn't have described Trudy that way, but I put that aside to concentrate on the other thing Jan had said. "She'd been having someone over?"

"Yes. A number of evenings around the time she died."

Trudy had never mentioned she was having someone over. I'd been under the impression she limited her visitors. I was one of the few allowed into her "inner sanctum." She and I had been alike that way.

"Do you know who her visitor was?" I asked.

"No. It was always too dark for me to see. Her front light had burned out. But Rosie started barking at seven every night, so I'm pretty sure it was the same person who came each time."

"Did you tell the police that?"

"We did, although there wasn't much to tell. We didn't have a license plate number or anything."

Stewart came running over to us. Jan put her arm around him and pulled him close.

"What are you guys talking about?" he asked, squirming out of her hold.

Jan said, "The person Trudy was having over. I was telling Kayla that we couldn't see who it was."

"I saw their car."

"You did?" Jan and I said at the same time.

"It was a Mercedes like Dad's. I saw it driving away the night me and Dustin worked on our science project. Its taillight was busted."

"Are you sure it was a Mercedes? It must have been dark." The beach ball rolled over to us. Jan picked it up and threw it back to a girl wearing a baseball cap.

Stewart nodded.

"Did you happen to see the license plate number too?" I asked.

Stewart put his finger to his chin and tilted his head left and right. "I think there were a bunch of numbers and the letters 'DUS' like in 'Dustin.'" With that, he ran back to the trampoline.

"Don't know if that helps," Jan said to me. "It might have nothing to do with her murder."

"Yeah. But we should let the police know. I can do it."

As far as I knew, none of the other parents were friends or neighbors of Trudy's. I didn't think any more information would be forthcoming.

After we ate sandwiches and chips and the cake was cut, I snagged a piece for Tristan and made my good-byes.

On the way home, I unearthed Brian's card from my messenger bag and called him. I told him about the Mercedes, admitting that a seven-year-old had come up with the information, which might have lessened its impact. He nevertheless made a note of it, but also reminded me I wasn't a detective and I should keep out of the investigations, thank you very much.

I was distracted by what Jan had said about Trudy and almost tripped over a rock on the coastal path. I couldn't imagine her arguing with anyone. She was so soft-spoken and gentle. But a barking dog could have sent me over the edge too. Although I liked dogs, barking was in my top ten of annoying noises.

Then I remembered Jan saying the dog incident wasn't the first time she and her husband had differences with Trudy. What else could they have been at odds about? Had the Williamses taken matters into their own hands to end the ongoing conflict? I doubted Jan and Austin were killers, but I wanted to ask Isabella what she thought.

After dropping off the slice of dessert to Tristan, I went inside my cottage and got to work on a cake for a christening. Business was good.

MY MOM CALLED THAT EVENING to formally invite me for Christmas. We'd already tentatively agreed that I'd drive up to Springvale in the Bay Area on Christmas Eve, stay the night, and spend Christmas Day with her and my stepdad, Bob.

"Looking forward to it, Mom," I said. "I'll get an early start on Christmas Eve."

I hadn't told my mother yet that Trudy had been murdered, let alone that I was actively investigating the crime. I didn't want her to worry about me, so I decided not to bring it up for now.

"Those pictures you sent of Sugar are simply adorable," Mom said. "I'm glad you have a furry companion again. I know how you miss Callie." Callie was the calico cat Mom and I adopted after she separated from my dad and we were on our own.

"I can't wait to see her," I said. "And you guys, too, of course."

I promised to send more pictures soon, both of Sugar and of the desserts I was working on, and we said good-bye.

ON MONDAY, I WENT TO THE CLUBHOUSE RESTAURANT to talk to Isabella after delivering my cake for the christening. She brought me a decaf caramel latte and I told her what Jan Williams had said at the birthday party.

"It can't have been Jan or Austin," she said. "Trudy was killed sometime around three, right?"

"Right." I'd looked at the clock when Trudy called me at two thirty, and I'd found her at three thirty.

"They were here for a long lunch that day. I remember because Austin was drinking and got a little flirty. I don't think they left until four. I was going to tell you about it when you came in, but of course you had bigger things on your mind."

"He flirted with you with Jan right there?"

"It happens." She gave me a self-satisfied smile.

"Well, what about what Jan said? You knew Trudy longer than I did." I cupped my hands around my coffee cup. "Am I missing something from her personality? As far as I'm concerned, she was sweet, gentle, and non-confrontational. Into knitting and cookies. Playing Scrabble."

Isabella laughed. "Kayla, come on. People are complex. And remember her age. Who knows what she was like when she was younger? In fact, something from her past might tie into her murder. She had a lot of years in which she could have made an enemy or two."

I considered Isabella's suggestion. "Okay, who would know?"

"Stanley Young would be a good bet. They'd been friends for years."

"Good thinking. I remember her talking about him. I actually met him when I did the desserts for a block party last month. He lives in that cute sea-green house at Seashell Street and Sea Lion Drive. I'll go over and see him." Maybe if I found out more about Trudy's past, I'd discover who had a motive to kill her. Stanley would be a good start.

STANLEY WASN'T THE MOST TRUSTING PERSON I'd ever met. He eventually invited me in, after asking for my name, age, height, and social security number. It probably wasn't that bad, but I did feel as though I were applying for the CIA or FBI. He didn't remember meeting me at the block party.

He directed me to sit on a beaten-up couch, while he took a seat in a lounge chair. An older yellow Labrador padded over and lay at his feet.

"This is Beau," Stanley said as he adjusted his hearing aids. "We're the same age. Ninety-one. We're all we have left in the world."

"Hi, Beau."

Beau slowly rose and came over to me. I gave him my hand to sniff and he licked it.

"Aww, hi, cutie." I fondled his ears and scratched his head.

"You like dogs?" Stanley took the throw that was folded over his chair and spread it across his legs.

"I like most animals. I recently acquired a cat. Well, it's Sugar. Trudy's cat. I took her in . . ." I hesitated.

"You don't need to say it. I know all about what happened. They have any leads?"

I shook my head. "That's what's so strange. It wasn't a burglary. Do you have any thoughts? She was such a sweet and quiet person. I don't know why anyone would hurt her."

Stanley laughed so hard that I feared he'd have a heart attack. Beau looked up at him in alarm.

"Are you kidding me? I knew Trudy for decades. She was one wild woman. More relationships than I can count. Men and a couple of women too. Vandalism, drugs, drinking to excess; you name it, Trudy tried it. She was one of those 'I'll do anything once' types."

Now I was the one in danger of having a heart attack. This didn't sound like the Trudy I knew and loved. Later, I would have to figure out how to take in this information, but for now I had questions.

I asked, "Do you think someone from her past might have killed her?"

"Possible."

"Any ideas?"

"No. You'll have to skedaddle now. It's time for Beau and me to go on our daily constitutional."

It was an abrupt end to our conversation, but I went with it. "Okay. Well, thanks for talking with me."

"Be careful," he said as I was leaving. He closed the door before I could ask what he meant. I'd managed to convince myself what I was doing wasn't dangerous. Talking to people about Trudy's death wasn't any different from meeting with a client who wanted to commission a cake. And yet . . . I couldn't ignore the fact I might one day come face to face with Trudy's killer.

CHAPTER 4

MANAGING MY BUSINESS, INVESTIGATING TRUDY'S MURDER, taking care of a cat, and going on first dates was creating a time crunch for me. I'd been planning to update my website with recent pictures of my desserts, send out invoices, and order new blue bakery boxes, but I'd accomplished none of it. The day after I met with Stanley, I went into my office to work, determined to get lots done. I hadn't made much progress when the sound of Sugar's mewing drifted into the office. The mewing turned to meowing and the meowing turned to whining.

"I'm in here, sweetheart," I called out, and she ambled into the room. After circling my chair a few times, she jumped on my desk and lay squarely across my to-do list. I could have sworn a smug smile crossed her face.

I went in search of something that could distract her. I found a plastic ball among her toys, brought it back into the office, and rolled it across the floor. Intrigued by the jangling sound it made, Sugar jumped down from the desk and batted the ball, then went skittering across the wood floor into the hallway after it. With her busy, I returned to my tasks.

THE BUSINESS PHONE RANG AS I was finishing my work. It was Jason.

After a few pleasantries, he said, "Your cakes are a big hit. I already need to place another order. Can I have two more chocolate cakes and try a couple of apple pies?"

"Of course. I can get them to you tomorrow afternoon."

"Perfect. Now, is it all right to bring up a personal matter on your business line again?" I could hear the smile in his voice.

"Yes, I suppose," I said. "But this is the last time."

"May I take you to dinner on Thursday?"

"I'd like that." We arranged the place and the time, and we hung up.

The idea of seeing Jason for another date stirred up some feelings of apprehension as well as pleasant anticipation. I needed a walk to clear my head.

After confirming Sugar was now snoozing on the bed, I took to the coastal path. A pleasant breeze caressed my face as I gazed at the colorful ice plant to the side of the trail. While I was admiring their pink flowers, I heard voices raised ahead of me. I stopped, not wanting to invade anyone's privacy.

"Where *are* they?"

"I don't know. I'm sorry."

"Don't be sorry. Tell me what you're going to do about it."

A bicycle whirring past kept me from hearing the rest of the conversation, but I could have sworn I heard the name "Trudy."

I approached the location where I'd heard the voices. The two people were gone. No doubt they'd headed down to the water, where dozens of beach-goers were availing themselves of the sun and sand. The day was unseasonably warm for November in Central California.

Who were the people I'd overheard? *Had* they been talking about Trudy? *My* Trudy? It wasn't a particularly popular name. I hadn't come across any other Trudys in our community. Although I hadn't caught every word of the conversation, it was clear from the tones of voice that the discussion had been heated. Was it possible the two knew something about her murder? Could they have been involved?

WHEN I RETURNED HOME, SUGAR SAT ON MY LAP while I went over what I'd learned from my investigations so far. Trudy had been—in Stanley Young's words—a wild woman when she was younger, a potential cheater at bingo when older, and had sparred with Austin Williams over a barking dog shortly before her death. Two people who may or may not have had something to do with her murder may or may not have been talking about her on the coastal walk. She'd been having someone over frequently before she died, someone who drove a Mercedes with a broken taillight. She hadn't been burgled, and on the day of her death, she came home early. Disparate pieces of information that didn't add up to much of anything at all.

I sighed, feeling frustrated. I was glad I baked for a living.

Sugar looked up at me and we exchanged a nose kiss.

"You're such a sweet girl," I told her as I scratched her ears. "You're my new best pal. I don't think Iz will mind."

Thinking about friends reminded me that Trudy had lived the last few months of her life without any family. When her sister died at the age of ninety-three, Trudy told me she was the last standing Dillingham. She hadn't sounded aggrieved. She was content to have me as well as her friends at the senior center for companions.

A tear ran down my cheek. Trudy had been a happy person in good health. Had she known she didn't have much time left? I was determined to find out who had ended her life.

I HADN'T HAD A CHANCE TO SEE ISABELLA for a few days, so a week after Trudy's death, I called and invited her over for a cake tasting.

An engaged couple had ordered a beach-themed wedding cake but assigned me the task of deciding on the flavor and design. The bride had told me she was tired of making decisions. Apparently, she and her fiancé weren't dessert lovers and didn't care much about the cake. I didn't mind. Eating a bunch of cake with my best friend wasn't exactly a hardship.

Sugar delayed us, insisting both Isabella and I snuggle her and play with her for about a half hour. Isabella was as enamored with her as I. We finally made it into the kitchen with the pocket door firmly closed.

As I placed slivers of cake with a variety of non-perishable fillings onto two plates, I updated Isabella on the argument I'd overheard on the coastal walk as well as the conversation with Stanley. Periodically, Sugar came to the door and meowed, but we told her to amuse herself.

"Can you believe it, Iz? Drugs, drinking, numerous relationships? My sweet and innocent Trudy."

"Let me ask you something. If you had known all that, would you not have been friends with her?"

Her question gave me pause. I liked to think of myself as open-minded, and perhaps I was, but I had considered Trudy a grandmother figure. I wasn't comfortable learning that my stand-in grandparent might not have been as innocent as I'd believed.

Isabella snapped her fingers in front of my face. "Earth to Kayla. You haven't answered my question."

"I don't think anything would have changed had I known," I said. "It's just so weird to think of her that way. Meanwhile, I'm no closer to knowing who killed her. We know it wasn't Jan or Austin, despite their ongoing disagreements with her, whatever those were. I wonder about the person who'd been visiting her. Was it the killer? Who were the people I overheard on the trail? Is it possible one of them did it? I don't know where to go from here."

"Brian said this morning he and his partner are coming up empty too. Not that I'm supposed to be telling you."

"Right. My lips are sealed." I glanced at the cupcake-shaped clock on the wall. "Shoot. Hurry up and taste these so I can decide. I've gotta get ready to go soon."

"Got a delivery?"

"Um, no." I busied myself tasting a slice of lemon cake. "Hmm. This one is good. A top contender, for sure."

"Where are you going, then?" Isabella asked.

I chewed and swallowed. "Okay, I guess it's time to tell you, but I don't want you to go crazy when I do. I seem to be . . . dating."

"Way to bury the lede. Who is it? How did this happen? When did this happen? Why didn't you tell me?"

"His name is Jason Banks. He owns Fishes Do Come True down at the wharf. I met him last week. He invited me out for last Saturday night and again for tonight. Please don't give me that excited look. I don't want it to be a big deal. I have my hands full with the business, Sugar, and my investigations."

"Kayla." Isabella pulled me toward her into a quick hug. Like Trudy, she was ultra-aware of my personal space. "This is wonderful. I'm so proud of you. Giving love another chance."

"No one said anything about love. Dial it down."

"What does he look like? Is he cute?"

"Yes, he's very cute. Dark hair, blue eyes. Clean-shaven. Tall but not too tall."

"He sounds divine." She looked me over. "Tell me you're not wearing that."

I glanced down at my jeans and sweater. "I was going to. Why?"

"Kayla. Honey. You're going on a date. It's okay to dress up a little."

"I don't have anything dressy. Last time I wore a shirt and jeans. A nice shirt. It felt right. Sugar approved." I took a bite of raspberry cake.

"You have skirts. I have seen them. You wore one to Selma Tillman's wedding."

I shook my head. "I don't think I want to wear a skirt. It's chilly today."

"There's this new invention you might not have heard of. They're called tights. They keep you warm. If you don't have any, they are easy to come by."

"I don't like tights. They're scratchy and itchy. I couldn't stand them when I was a kid."

"They've come a long way since then. I'm gonna run over to my house and I'll be right back. You're going to wear a skirt and tights on this date and you're going to look adorable."

"You didn't finish tasting the cakes. I need help figuring out the best one."

"Give me a doggie bag. I'll decide in the car."

I did as she said, but I felt she wasn't going to perform due diligence. I decided to go with the raspberry cake. It was tasty, and the red would be ideal for the December wedding next month. I stored the leftovers and cleaned the kitchen.

ISABELLA RETURNED SOON with a long-sleeved blue dress, high heels, a purse . . . and no mention of the cakes. I was glad I'd made the decision on my own. At least she hadn't brought tights.

I usually didn't enjoy dressing up, but I liked what Isabella had brought. "Thanks, Iz."

"I'll help with your makeup too."

"You're the best."

She came up to me and stared into my face, making me squirm. "You have such beautiful eyes. Let's lose the glasses. You have contacts, don't you?"

"I do. I hardly ever wear them. The glasses are more comfortable."

"But for a date, you can stand them, right? Please?"

"Yeah, okay. I'll go put them in."

Fifteen minutes later, Isabella said my brown eyes were popping with the contacts in, and a nice contrast to my blond hair that she'd expertly styled into soft curls. Once I was dressed and Isabella had gone to town with eye makeup and lipstick, she gave me a thumbs-up. We went our separate ways—she to work and me to the wharf.

Despite being on the late side, I beat Jason to Sam's and nabbed a table on the deck. A few minutes later, he came outside, looked around, and went back inside. Apparently, he didn't recognize me. I hurried after him and touched his back. He turned around.

"Kayla, it's you. You look . . . different. I didn't recognize you."

"It's too much, isn't it? I don't feel like myself at all."

"Don't get me wrong. You look beautiful, but I like the understated look you had before too."

"Is 'understated' your way of saying 'blah and boring'?"

"Not at all. Look, you're very pretty whatever you do. I don't like to dress up, so I kind of like it when my girlfriends don't either. Otherwise, I come off looking like a slob." He laughed.

"Girlfriend?" Heat suffused my face.

"Oh. No, I didn't mean to imply—"

"It's okay. I like it."

"I do too. Maybe it's a little soon, but let's take it for a spin. So, come on, girlfriend, let's go reclaim that table before someone grabs it."

We both ordered grilled filet of sole and french fries. Conversation was easy as we discussed baseball and a little politics. Fortunately, the only argument involved which baseball teams we liked. Jason was originally from Chicago, so he was Cubs all the way. As a native of the San Francisco Bay Area, I preferred the Giants and A's.

"What about your family?" Jason asked. "You haven't mentioned your parents or any siblings."

"I'm an only child. My parents divorced when I was seventeen. My mom and I moved into an apartment, she and my father sold the house I grew up in, and Dad moved to Florida. Mom remarried a couple of years later. She and my stepdad live in a townhouse in Springvale, my hometown."

"Do you see them?"

"My mom and stepfather? Yeah, every couple of months. I miss not being closer to them, though. What about you? Parents? Siblings other than Paula?"

"The folks are alive and well in Chicago. They divorced when I was ten. I moved out here after college and raved about it so much to Paula that she followed me out a year later. She's my only sibling."

I nodded, and we looked out at the ocean. The full moon cast a pretty glow over the water.

"It's so beautiful here, isn't it?" I said.

"Honestly, I can't imagine a nicer place," Jason agreed. "Tell me more. How did you get started in baking?"

"When I moved down here, I was looking for something creative to do. I'd always loved baking with my mom. She gave me the seed money and recipes to get my business going."

"Do you love it?"

I laughed. "I do now, yes. The first year was incredibly stressful. Classes, permits, inspections. Consultations with attorneys and accountants. I almost gave up half a dozen times. But everyone was so supportive. My friend Isabella was great. Trudy too." I let a beat go by. "I miss her so much."

He patted my hand.

"My landlord, Tristan, was also a big help. He spoke on my behalf to the Seaside Shores Board of Directors and convinced them to allow me to operate out of my home. He let me remodel the kitchen, too, to maximize the space."

"You have a lot of people who care about you."

I nodded as a warm feeling enveloped me. I knew how fortunate I was.

Jason and I had become comfortable enough with each other that he grabbed some fries from my plate and I stole the sourdough bread he hadn't touched. But after nearly two hours, my eyes felt gritty from the contacts and my head ached. As much as I liked Jason, I didn't want to talk anymore. It was time for me to go home to a quiet room and read a book.

I explained all this to Jason when he suggested we walk on the beach once we'd left the restaurant.

"I totally get it. My sis is the same way. After a certain amount of time, she's done. Some days are worse than others. May I call you tomorrow, though?"

"Yes, that would be great, and thanks for dinner. It was fun."

He leaned in and gave me a swift kiss on the mouth. It was just right. Then he drove me home and gave me another quick kiss before I went inside.

THE NEXT AFTERNOON, I TOOK THREE APPLE PIES to the clubhouse restaurant. Whenever I had a cancellation, I donated the desserts to the restaurant so they wouldn't go to waste. I'd just finished baking the pies that morning when my client called to say she had the flu and her big family gathering wasn't happening.

Isabella's boss, Vincent, steadfastly refused to make me his go-to baker, though he never turned down my donations. I hoped he'd order from me someday, but Isabella had told me he was resistant to change and I shouldn't hold my breath.

Isabella wasted no time in cutting into one of the pies and bringing two slices to a table overlooking the water, where we settled in.

Vincent, who was adding fresh flowers to the tables, threw her a look. She shook her head and mouthed, "Break." He sighed and ran his hand across his bald head.

I wasn't sure why he cared so much. There were very few people in the restaurant at that hour. It was the no-man's land between lunch and dinner. The other waitress on duty, Daisy, was combining catsup bottles across the room.

"Iz, I don't want to get you into trouble."

"Seriously, Kayla. He's not gonna fire me. My friend brings him pies free of charge. And, more importantly, I'm the best waitress he's ever had."

Isabella had earned her self-confidence the hard way. Originally from Los Angeles, she lost both her parents to a car accident when she was thirteen. She went to live with an aunt she barely knew. While many teenagers might have spiraled downward from there, Isabella studied hard and received a full ride to UC Oceanville. Her part-time job at the clubhouse was meant to end after graduation, but she decided to stay on full-time, eventually renting a house in the community close to work. She was diligent about putting money away for law school and had started studying for the admission test. She had zero doubts she would pass the LSAT with flying colors, get into a top law school, and become a successful lawyer specializing in women's rights.

Even though my business was doing well, and I received almost one hundred percent positive feedback, it was hard to sell myself. I knew I could take a page from Isabella's book.

"This is sooo good," Isabella moaned. She'd already eaten half her slice. "Why aren't you eating?"

"I don't know. I'm full from last night, I guess. I ate a lot."

"I can't believe I forgot to ask. Your scrumptious pie distracted me. How was the big date? Did he love the clothes and the makeup?"

"He said I looked pretty but he likes if I don't dress up. He usually dresses casually. Which is good, because I do like to be comfortable."

Isabella frowned at me. "Moving on. How was the date itself?"

"Dinner was very nice, but I kind of maxed out on the whole thing. We didn't walk on the beach like he wanted."

"Did he kiss you?"

"Yes. Please don't go crazy."

She got up and did a little dance. Vincent glowered at her while I blushed.

I pulled her back into her chair. "Stop it. I want to ask you something. Any ideas who I could talk to next? Or should I go back to Stanley? I feel like he had more to say, but he cut me off."

"You could go see him again."

"I'm afraid he'll tell me something else I don't want to hear, but I know I might have to bite the bullet. Oh, Iz. I'm having such a difficult time squaring my Trudy with this Trudy I've been hearing about. Especially the young version."

"People change. Aren't you different now from when you were in your twenties and early thirties?"

"Yes and no. I've always been an introvert. I've never done anything wild, at least like what Stanley said Trudy did. I think as I've gotten older, I've become more introverted and my sensitivity has intensified."

"Or maybe you've given up a little? When's the last time you took a risk or went on an adventure?"

The suggestion gave me pause. Maybe I *wasn't* getting out of my comfort zone enough. Introverted HSPs often fell back on staying at home to avoid overstimulation, but that put them at risk of missing out on pleasurable new experiences. Still, wasn't I already out of my comfort zone by investigating Trudy's murder? I also had gone to dinner on my own and met Jason. Not only was I now dating him, he'd become a client. I said as much to Isabella.

"See? Good things *can* happen when you push yourself to try something new."

I remembered Trudy suggesting something similar. They might be right, but I also knew it was important to honor my HSP needs.

"Now, about me," Isabella said. "I met someone."

"Wait, what? I thought you were dating Brian."

"We never said we'd be exclusive. Jack just moved here. He came down to the restaurant for dinner last night. He's completely gorgeous. I introduced myself even though he was at Daisy's table."

"Iz, I can't believe you."

"It worked. We went out dancing at a club." She did a little cha-cha-cha in her seat.

"The same day you met?"

She nodded. "As soon as I was off work."

I couldn't even conceive of going to a club. Too many people, loud music, weird lighting. I hoped Jason would never suggest it.

"Are you going to tell Brian about Jack?" I asked.

"I don't think I have to since we never promised anything."

I marveled at my friend. Two boyfriends? One was enough for me. And I wasn't convinced one wasn't too much.

A few minutes later, Vincent caught Isabella's eye and tapped his watch. I paid my check, said good-bye to Isabella, and headed straight home to bake.

CHAPTER 5

THE NEXT MORNING, FINISHED WITH ONE BAKING PROJECT and poised to begin a second, I took a phone call from the attorney who'd advised me when I first opened my business. Theodore Patel had been Trudy's attorney for years, and she'd recommended him to me.

After he'd asked after my business, Patel informed me that Trudy's house would be sold and the proceeds disbursed to a number of animal shelters around the county. He confirmed what I already knew—Trudy had no remaining living relatives.

Patel went on to say that Trudy had wanted her ashes scattered in the ocean and had requested I take care of it. She'd been insistent there not be a memorial service. Everything had been arranged, and all I needed to do was pick up the ashes and rent a boat with funds she'd set aside.

"When did she arrange all of this with you?" I asked Patel.

"When she hired me. I believe she'd turned sixty-five the week before. She added the part about you about a year ago."

We said good-bye, and I hung up, thinking Trudy had done the responsible thing by seeing an attorney to ensure her wishes were carried out. I liked the idea of her remains going into the sea that she loved so much. I sat on the couch to draw up a to-do list and make a few phone calls.

THE NEXT AFTERNOON, I MET PATEL to collect Trudy's ashes and the required permit he'd already secured, then joined up with Jason and Isabella at a boat rental shop at the wharf. I'd booked a charter for two thirty.

The captain introduced himself as Tom and led us to the boat, where we met the crew and set sail about ten minutes later. The sun sparkled off the bluish-green water and I put on my clip-on sunglasses. Although a little chilly, the day was perfectly clear. Trudy would have loved it.

Once we were the required distance out, Jason, Isabella, and I each took a handful of Trudy's ashes and threw them into the water. Isabella had brought several different-colored gerberas—Trudy's favorite flower—so we offered those to the sea as well.

Isabella and I shared a few memories of Trudy as the boat circled the area. Some made us cry and others made us laugh uproariously. I told the story of the day Trudy and I drove out to the country in Ventana Valley to go apple picking. On the way home, on a deserted road, my mini-van broke down. I couldn't get cell service. We waited for a car to come by, and when one finally approached, Trudy rolled up the bottom of her pants and showed off her leg, Claudette Colbert-style. The car immediately stopped and picked us up. It turned out the driver was a good friend of Trudy's who would have stopped anyway, but Trudy *did* have very shapely legs.

When we were through sharing our memories, I whispered, my voice cracking, "Miss you, Trudy." Isabella and Jason put their arms around me and held me close. We stayed that way, in a group hug, for what seemed like hours, and I didn't find the extended contact overstimulating at all.

On dry land again, we went to Sam's for a late lunch/early dinner. We took a table on the deck and ordered crab cakes, oysters, and fish and chips. We were kept warm by the heaters and the jackets we'd worn for our trip out on the ocean.

There was an unspoken agreement that we wouldn't speak about Trudy or the circumstances of her death. We talked about food and movies, and I shared some of Sugar's latest antics, making us laugh. When the sun began its slow dive into the ocean, we grew quiet. We looked at each other and smiled. I knew we were all in agreement about how fleeting life was, yet amazing and lovely. Jason squeezed my hand, and a tear trickled down my face. My only wish was that Trudy could have been there with us, but then again, maybe she was.

THE NEXT DAY, I MADE A SMALL BATCH OF SUGAR COOKIES for my personal enjoyment, adding some raspberry filling in the centers. I tried one and stored the rest.

I'd just finished cleaning the kitchen and was on the couch petting Sugar when a light tap on the front door made us both look up. Sugar jumped down and ran to the door as if she were the proprietress of the establishment and not me. I scooped her into my arms and peered through the peephole. A woman who appeared to be in her early seventies stood on the porch.

I opened the door and let in my visitor, who was tall and trim with neatly-styled brown hair. She smiled at me, revealing adult braces. "Hello. I'm Nancy Dougherty. I was a friend of Trudy's from the senior center."

I put Sugar on the floor, and Nancy and I shook hands.

"Kayla Jeffries. Nice to meet you."

"I brought you the pictures I took with my camera on what turned out to be Trudy's last day at the center. I thought you might want them since your pie is front and center."

"Oh yes. Thank you so much."

She handed them over, bent to scratch under Sugar's chin, and said good-bye.

I took the pictures over to the couch. It was difficult to see Trudy on what I now knew was her last day of life, but nice too. She looked happy.

Seeing nothing that might help solve her murder, I put the photos aside. I wanted to go see Stanley Young again.

I put on a sweater and packed up a few cookies to offer Stanley in hopes of getting him to talk. Outside, I clipped my sunglasses over my frames and walked over to his street.

This time, I didn't even make it inside his house. He kept me standing on the rubber mat that read "Come In," a message I found sadly misleading.

"Sick. Horrible sore throat," he said in a raspy tone. "Can't have visitors." Before I could give him the cookies or even tell him to feel better, he shut the door. But not before I'd caught sight of a bowl of pretzels on the table near his chair. Who ate pretzels when they had a sore throat? Was he lying? If so, why?

I trundled down to the clubhouse restaurant and asked Isabella to join me for a coffee. Vincent wasn't around, so she could take a break without him staring her down.

We sat at a table overlooking the water and sipped our lattes. I updated Isabella on the pictures from Nancy as well as the pretzels and Stanley's refusal to let me in. "What do you think, Iz?"

"It definitely sounds like he knows more than he's letting on. I'll ask Brian if they've talked to him. He might be more forthcoming with the police."

"Maybe."

"The other possibility is . . ."

"What?" I asked.

"He saw your reaction when he told you about Trudy's wildness and is reluctant to upset you further. That might be why he cut you off the first time you saw him."

I nodded. "That could be."

"By the way, did you ask Nancy if she had any ideas about who the killer is? It sounds like she might have known Trudy pretty well."

"Oh shoot, I should have. She left her contact information on the envelope of pictures. I'll give her a call after I finish baking a cake for an anniversary party. In fact, I better go get started."

At home, once I'd wrapped up the order, I tried to reach Nancy but didn't get an answer. The number was probably a landline without voice mail, putting her somewhere in the 1970s in terms of technology. It reminded me of Trudy, who had refused to get a computer, a cell phone, or even an e-reader—even though I told her she could enlarge the font on the latter to make reading easier on her eyes. I scribbled a reminder on a sticky note to try Nancy again later.

I made a sandwich and went into the office to work on my website. Before bed, I talked to Jason on the phone. We had one of those exchanges in which he told me to hang up first and I told *him* to hang up first. Feeling happy but sleepy, I finally said I had to go. Sugar curled up at the foot of the bed and I fell asleep to the sound of rain on the roof, my favorite sound in the world.

THE NEXT MORNING, THE WEATHER HAD CLEARED and the air smelled delicious from the rain. After I'd delivered the anniversary cake to Sandpiper Lane, a few blocks away, I went back home. I tried Nancy again but didn't reach her.

Stumped on where to go next with my investigations, I decided to treat myself to a couple of hours at the Oceanville Aquarium. Maybe my subconscious would come up with an idea while I was doing something else, like when I had a baking conundrum.

I strolled through the aquarium, in awe of the fish and octopuses and general amazingness of the sea. I especially enjoyed the special penguin exhibit and immediately had the urge to make a black and white cake, part vanilla and part chocolate. When I got the chance, I'd look for a penguin-shaped pan online.

At my last stop, the otter enclosure, I recognized one of Trudy's friends whom I'd met the previous year at Seaside Shores's holiday party. She stood beside a child who looked to be seven or eight. I went over.

"Vicky? Kayla Jeffries. We met last year at the holiday party?"

"Hi, Kayla. Sure, I remember you. This is my daughter, Angie."

Angie looked up at me with soft brown eyes and pulled a piece of curly blond hair into her mouth.

"Hi, Angie," I said. "It's so nice to meet you. I don't think I saw you at the party last year."

"I was sick."

"Oh, I'm sorry. I'm sure you'll make it this year. Are you enjoying the aquarium?"

"Uh, huh." She reached around to the back of her neck and scratched.

"Label?" I asked.

She nodded solemnly. "Mom keeps saying she'll cut it out, but she forgets."

Vicky looked sheepish.

"How do you feel about tights?" I asked Angie next.

She screwed up her mouth in a pout and shook her head. She turned away to the otters.

"Vicky, is Angie sensitive to harsh lighting and strong smells too?"

"Yes. How did you know?"

"Give me your email address and I'll send you some information. I'm an HSP—highly sensitive person—and I think your daughter might be too. Things that don't bother other people bother us a whole lot. We take in too much input, like smells, sights, and sounds. And people's emotions, as well."

"I've never heard of it, but I'd love the information. It sounds just like her. She always knows when something's bothering me. She's also so sweet with things she likes. She nuzzles our cat's head and digs her toes into the sand at the beach. She gets positively euphoric."

"HSPs can be very drawn to nature and animals."

Vicky wrote down her email address on her aquarium brochure. We checked out Angie. She was still enthralled by the otters.

"Awful about Trudy, wasn't it?" Vicky said quietly. "Angie doesn't know yet. I hate to break it to her. They bonded a couple of years ago when her class read to seniors at the center. We'd visit her every so often."

"Yes, it was horrible. I found her."

Vicky grimaced and placed her hand on mine.

"The police aren't getting very far with solving the crime," I told her. "Can you think of anything that could be helpful?"

Vicky considered. "I know she had an ongoing feud with some neighbors."

"Austin and Jan Williams?"

"No. Topher and Laura Fremont. Something about the trees in her backyard blocking their view, I think. Unfortunately, that kind of disagreement can sometimes get out of hand."

"Okay. I'll check it out. Thanks."

I told the two good-bye and stopped by the gift shop on the way out. I bought Jason a mug with an otter on it and found a pretty seashell hair clip for Isabella.

As I drove home, I thought about what Vicky had said. Maybe it was Laura and Topher I'd overheard on the coastal walk and they'd been arguing about something related to the murder.

AT HOME, I SHUT MYSELF IN THE KITCHEN to make a peppermint cream pie. I wasn't allowed to sell anything perishable that had to be refrigerated, but I liked to make cream pies in an unofficial capacity. I hoped Trudy had sampled the pie I'd given her the day she died. It was my go-to holiday dessert for friends and family, and she'd always loved it.

I ground chocolate cookies into small pieces, added butter, and formed the crust. I didn't have time to make my filling from scratch today, so while the crust baked, I whipped up instant vanilla pudding from a box, adding a crushed-up miniature candy cane to the mixture. When the crust was ready, I poured in the pudding and set the pie in the refrigerator. I whipped my cream, again including a miniature candy cane. Once I'd covered the pie in cream and sprinkled crushed candy canes on top, I added some chocolate seashells.

I checked in the community directory for the Fremonts' address and discovered they lived on a street above Trudy's. I set out on foot. Finding myself out of breath as I climbed the hill on Otter Street, I decided I really needed to amp up my exercise. Leisurely walks along the coastal path weren't cutting it.

Taking note of the Honda in the Fremonts' driveway—definitely not a Mercedes—I approached the front door. I announced my arrival with a knocker shaped like an anchor, which I immediately wished I owned.

Laura, who looked to be in her mid-fifties, invited me in after I'd introduced myself and given her the pie. The dessert had the desired effect of bringing out her friendliness, which could work to my advantage.

As I stood in the foyer, she put the pie in the fridge and didn't suggest we have some. She directed me into the living room where we each took a chair. Laura sank into her seat and bent each wrist backward and forward as if in pain. I suspected she had arthritis. I remembered my late grandmother doing the same thing.

After a few minutes of chit-chat about the weather and the upcoming holidays, I said, "I found Trudy Dillingham after she was killed. I understand you and your husband had a little disagreement with her over the trees in her backyard. They were blocking your view?"

"It wasn't the trees. She was planning on building some atrocious addition. An observatory or something like that." She looked over to the picture window on the west side of the room and I rose to go peer out.

The window offered, at the moment, a lovely view of the ocean. But Trudy's backyard was indeed in the line of sight. Depending on the size and location, an exterior building in the yard could seriously impair the Fremonts' view. An observatory? Another thing Trudy had never mentioned to me.

I returned to my chair. "I can see why you'd be upset. I'd hate anything blocking my view. The association wouldn't have approved an observatory, would they?" Like most homeowner associations, Seaside Shores enforced various rules and regulations to safeguard a specific look of the community and to ensure residents didn't pose a nuisance to their neighbors.

"She had some kind of in with the board. They'd approved it already," Laura answered.

I'd been listening carefully to her voice. Was she one half of the couple I'd heard that day on the coastal walk? I couldn't be sure.

Laura was now frowning at me. I had a feeling the pie wasn't going to make up for how this conversation was going.

"Oh, I get it now," she said. "You're thinking either I or my husband killed her so the thing would never be constructed? I think you better leave now."

She escorted me to the door and out onto the stone walkway. My pie was not returned.

On the way home—a much easier walk since it was downhill—I reviewed the conversation. I'd learned another new thing about Trudy in addition to the fact she'd commissioned an observatory. She'd had an "in," as Laura called it, with someone on Seaside Shores's board of directors. I hadn't been aware she'd known someone on the board. Maybe all of these surprises about her would eventually lead me to finding out who had disliked her so much to kill her.

I'd gotten a good look at Laura's hands as I left and seen joint deformities and swelling. I questioned her ability to strangle Trudy. Her husband, however, might be another matter.

At home, I gave Sugar a few treats. While she ate, I looked up Topher Fremont on the internet and found out he was a librarian at the Oceanville Library. I located the car keys and drove over.

The teenager stationed at the library's front desk pointed to the reference area across the room when I asked to speak with Topher.

Topher stood when I approached the reference desk. The top of his dark hair was pulled back into a short ponytail and he wore a golden hoop in one ear. He smiled at me welcomingly.

I smiled back. "Hi, I'm Kayla Jeffries. You're Topher?"

"Yes."

I put my hand forward and we shook. I picked up a scent of a pleasant fruity cologne.

"I have a question about Trudy Dillingham," I said. "She was your neighbor?"

The smile left his face. "That's right. She was. I was floored when I heard what happened to her."

"Yeah, I know what you mean. I was the one who found her."

He blew out a long breath. "That's rough."

"It was, yes. I understand she was building an observatory on her property?"

"True. I'm not into astronomy, but to each their own." He sat on the edge of the desk and crossed his arms over his chest.

"It was going to block your view. I would be pretty mad about that."

"Yeah, and my wife was up in arms about it. I'm more of a live and let live kind of guy. Your home is your castle. You should be able to do anything you want. But my wife . . . she was upset. If she hadn't been here with our granddaughter for the reading-to-animals event, I might have suspected her." He laughed and pointed at a stack of flyers advertising the reading-to-animals program held every Thursday afternoon from 2-4. Yep, that covered the time Trudy was killed.

"You were here too?" I asked.

"Uh, huh. I have regular hours, as opposed to a lot of my co-workers. I'm here from nine to five Monday through Friday."

Sounded like an airtight alibi. "Thanks," I said. "I'm gonna go browse."

He nodded and turned to an approaching patron.

I left for the stacks, thinking that Topher hadn't even questioned why I was asking him about the observatory. His alibi could easily be checked, so I crossed him off my mental list of suspects and checked out a couple of cake decorating books, a few cozy mysteries, and a compilation of puzzles.

THE NEXT MORNING, BEFORE PLACING an order with my supplier, I lay on the couch with Sugar on my stomach and mulled over the alibis of my possible suspects. Austin, who'd argued with Trudy about his barking dog, had been at lunch with Jan at the clubhouse restaurant when the murder took place. Laura and Topher, whose view might have been blocked by Trudy's observatory, had both been at the library. Burton Engel, who was mad at Trudy for her bingo success, had been at the senior center. Everyone could account for their whereabouts at the time of her death.

Meanwhile, I was no closer to knowing the owner of the Mercedes nor the identity of the couple on the coastal walk. As for Stanley Young, he was worth pursuing for information. Did he know something he wasn't letting on? Maybe, but maybe not. It was all so impossible.

As I stroked Sugar's back, I was struck by an idea. In my first year of business, I'd designed a grid to keep track of which combinations of cakes, flavors, and fillings worked well together. A combination that was successful—such as chocolate cake with raspberry filling—received a checkmark, while one that didn't taste that good—lemon filling with chocolate frosting—garnered an X. The process had appealed to my puzzle-loving nature, reminding me of the logic problems I liked to solve when I was younger. Perhaps I could use the same technique for my investigations.

I put Sugar on the floor and went into the office for a pen and a piece of printer paper.

Back in the living room, I sat on the floor next to Sugar and made a grid for tracking suspects, means, motives, and opportunity. I began putting checkmarks and *X*'s into the grid according to what I knew. Anything I hadn't verified received a question mark, as did things I didn't understand yet.

Before I'd made much headway, I heard a noise outside which sounded like a meow. I put aside the grid to go open the front door. A woman in a business suit stood on the porch, holding . . . Sugar?

I whipped my head around. Sugar had jumped back onto the couch and was washing her paw. I snapped my head back to look at the woman. She was still holding a cat. A cat who looked like Sugar but who clearly *wasn't* Sugar.

The woman tried to get my attention by waving her hand in front of my face. "Hi, I'm Kellie Thompson. This is Sunflower. Your cat's sister?"

"Really?"

Sunflower struggled out of Kellie's hold and ran to the couch. Sugar jumped down. Seconds later, the two were licking each other and nuzzling each other's faces. Kellie and I made "awwing" noises.

"The mama cat had a small litter, just the two of them," Kellie said, tucking a stray piece of brown hair behind her ear. "Trudy and I each took one, but now my husband, daughter, and I are moving for my job. We're not allowed to have pets at the new place."

I nodded, sensing where this was going.

"Eileen Nichols told me you adopted Sugar and suggested you might consider taking in Sunflower. My daughter's terribly upset about the whole thing. I know she'd feel better knowing the two are together."

I looked at the two cats, who were now on the floor snuggling, their eyes half-closed in utter bliss. There seemed to be only one answer. "Sure."

"Thank you. That's a huge weight off my shoulders. Oh, I almost forgot. My daughter called her Flower for short and she responded to that."

"Flower is cute. Okay."

"I brought all her things. I'll get them from the car."

Five minutes later I said good-bye to Kellie, closed the door, and knelt to look at my two cats. Now that I could examine Sunflower up close, I saw she had golden eyes in contrast to Sugar's green ones. Otherwise, the white domestic shorthairs were identical; same color, size, and facial expressions.

Still snuggling, they looked up at me as if to say, "Isn't this the best thing ever?"

I had to agree that yes it was.

Eileen Nichols, Trudy's neighbor, called that evening and opened the conversation by asking about Sugar.

"She's great. I have Sunflower now too."

"I'm so glad that worked out," Eileen said. "Listen, a few of us met up with Trudy's lawyer and cleaned out her house after the police released it as a crime scene."

"You did? I could have helped. I'm sorry, I didn't know."

"Not to worry. I put a notice in the community newsletter after I heard from the lawyer. He said Trudy had wanted her neighbors to do it. Maybe she thought it would be too difficult for you, since you were so close."

"That was thoughtful of her," I said. "She was right I'd feel that way."

"We found a scrapbook. It has a lot of pictures and mementos from her past. It might help you. Since you're investigating her death, I mean."

Surprised, I asked, "You knew?"

"Yes. It's gotten around."

"Do you think I could take a look at it?"

"I'll bring it by tomorrow afternoon. I think it would be all right if you keep it."

"That would be perfect. I live in the cottage behind the home at the corner of Sea Lion Drive and Ocean Lane. Thanks so much."

As promised, Eileen brought by Trudy's scrapbook the next afternoon. I thanked her and sent her off with a few sugar cookies.

I sat on the couch to examine the book. It was stuffed with pressed flowers, programs, and menus, as well as dozens of pictures. I paged through photographs of Trudy as a child: scrawny and wet outside of a pool, her arm slung over the shoulders of a girl I guessed to be her sister; jumping rope with friends; eating cake at a birthday party. Next were pictures of her in college: playing tennis and at a sorority party. Shots of her in London as a young woman made me jealous: hamming it up next to a guard at Buckingham Palace, pointing to the original *Alice in Wonderland* in the British Museum, pretending to steal a portrait of

Shakespeare from The National Portrait Gallery.

There were also plenty of pictures of her at Seaside Shores; the two of us at the holiday party, shots at the senior center, a group photo of the knitting club.

I came upon a picture of Sugar and Sunflower as kittens. I removed the picture and laid it aside to put on the fridge.

Threaded throughout the scrapbook were pictures of Trudy with a man I recognized as Lars Chapman, the long-term mayor of Oceanville, at different stages in their lives. I knew she was an ardent supporter of his, but they seemed especially friendly with each other. Lars and his wife lived in Seaside Shores, so perhaps he and Trudy had gotten to know each other through some event or another.

I placed the book on the coffee table as a stab of longing for my friend went through me, accompanied by a feeling of frustration for not getting any answers. Would I ever discover who had killed Trudy?

CHAPTER 6

TWO DAYS AFTER HER ARRIVAL, Sunflower had settled in nicely. As I brainstormed how to create a cake shaped like a fish for a gender reveal party, I cuddled her in my arms, every so often bending to give her a kiss on the top of her head. Sugar sat companionably next to us on the couch. For each kiss Sunflower got, Sugar received a scratch under her chin.

"I have an idea," I said to Sunflower. "Your old family called you Flower, but I'm going to rename you Flour. It's different even though it sounds the same. You and your sister can be Sugar and Flour."

I'd have to take a picture of the cats together and post it to my website. My clients would get a kick out of their baking-themed names. For now, I went into the kitchen to prepare Jason's new order of cakes and apple pies.

LATER THAT AFTERNOON, AFTER DROPPING OFF JASON'S ORDER and getting a few kisses of my own, I got home to find the cats chasing each other through the house, bumping into things, batting toys, skittering across the wood floors, and generally making a racket.

"Hey, you two. This is too loud." But my rant ended in a giggle when Sugar tried to jump from the couch to the easy chair, missed, and dropped to the floor. In typical feline fashion, she acted as if she'd intended to fall all along, and she left the room to pursue Flour down the hallway.

With the two engaged, I took the opportunity to shut myself in the kitchen and make the fish-shaped cake for the gender reveal party. I'd deliver it before my date with Jason that evening.

The mom-to-be had requested a pink cake since she was having a girl. I got to work, creating an ombre effect by tinting each layer of the cake a progressively darker pink.

I made a vanilla frosting which I also colored pink. After the layers had cooked and cooled, I used a triangle cookie cutter to carve out the fish's mouth from each round. I sliced each cut-out piece in half and put aside the halves for the fins. I spread raspberry filling in between the layers and frosted the top, leaving the sides bare to show off the ombre look. Then I attached the fins and added the fondant eye and teeth I'd made earlier while preparing Jason's order. Satisfied with the result, I got ready to go.

"Hey, when's your birthday?" Jason asked as we chowed down on a shrimp pizza that evening at Luigi's in downtown Oceanville.

I finished chewing. Some people might consider shrimp on a pizza an odd choice, but it was the perfect match for the Alfredo sauce and mozzarella cheese. "I can't believe we haven't talked about our birthdays," I said. "Mine's October tenth. It was fun in 2010 because it was on ten-ten-ten. When's yours?"

"November twenty-first."

"Uh, November twenty-first as in the day after tomorrow?" I reached across the table and pushed gently against his arm. "You never told me."

"No need to make a fuss. I'm going to be at work, anyway. Because of your lovely self, I haven't been clocking my usual hours."

"At the very least you must have a cake. Your favorite is red velvet, right?"

"Right."

We continued eating pizza, but now my mind was on Jason's cake, and he had to get my attention several times. I was busy creating his cake in my head and it was hard to let it go.

After Jason drove me home, I went into the kitchen and shut the door. A little of this, a little of that, and soon I had my ingredients for a test cake and an idea for its shape. I started in.

Sugar and Flour began making a racket outside the kitchen. I peeked out and saw they were batting around the plastic ball I'd brought home with Sugar's things. The ball jangled every time they pawed at it. It was hard to concentrate on my measuring, but I couldn't bear to make them stop. They were the cutest things.

As I put the cake part of Jason's test dessert in the oven, I listened to the cats playing and felt a rush of love for them. I couldn't believe I'd ever resisted the idea of having a cat. The two added a dimension to my life I had never imagined. I hadn't even known I needed them. Dating Jason was going well too. If I could only solve Trudy's murder and put that behind me, life could be pretty good. I might even enter one of those competitions Trudy had encouraged me to try. It could be a way for me to honor her in my life.

THE NEXT DAY, I MADE JASON'S OFFICIAL BIRTHDAY CAKE and prepared two dozen chocolate cupcakes topped with white chocolate seashells for a ninetieth birthday party at the senior center. I delivered the order around noon and was surprised when a guest came up to me, introduced herself as Cynthia Amandoli, and asked about my investigations. Eileen was right— the news that I was looking into Trudy's murder had gotten around.

"My father dated Trudy after he divorced my mother in the early eighties," Cynthia said.

"No kidding? Do you think I could talk to him?" Maybe he would know if something from Trudy's past had anything to do with her murder.

"I don't see why not. He gets coffee at the Otter Café every day in downtown Oceanville. You can find him around nine each morning. He never misses his coffee. Oscar Lancaster is his name."

I thanked her, collected my payment for the cupcakes, and left.

The next morning, I tooled over to the Otter Café in my mini-van. I ordered a decaf latte at the counter. Once my drink was ready, I looked around and saw the most likely candidate to be Oscar—a heavyset man of Trudy's age, dressed smartly in an expensive-looking suit. I went over.

"I'd like another mocha, please," he said.

"Oh. I'm not a waitress." That's what I got for wearing black corduroy pants and a white blouse.

He waved his hand about. "Forgive me. What can I do for you?"

"Are you Oscar?"

"Guilty as charged."

"I was a friend of Trudy Dillingham's."

"I suppose you better sit down. What are you drinking?"

"A latte, but I already have one," I said, holding up my cup. "I don't need another."

"Something to eat, then? I have money to spend."

"Thanks. That would be nice."

He went to the counter and I sat at his table to wait. He came back a minute later with two blueberry muffins and handed me one. I thanked him.

After taking a bite of muffin, I said, "I met your daughter Cynthia yesterday. She told me you dated Trudy. What was she like back then?"

Surely Stanley had been exaggerating when he described the Trudy of old. Now I would get the truth from someone who had been intimate with her. Oscar would say how quiet and introverted Trudy had been.

"She was fun. Lively. Up for anything. We dated for, I don't know, six or seven months."

"Oh." My heart sank. It was all true.

"She convinced me to break into Governor Alcott's office back in the early eighties," Oscar said.

A break-in? At the *governor's* office? "Why?"

"She disliked him. He was very anti-women's rights. She was quite the feminist."

Sounded like Isabella. "So you broke in? And did what?"

"Destroyed a painting, tore up his diplomas. Took files out of the filing cabinet and scattered them around the room." His mouth turned down in an expression of distaste.

Trudy's life was becoming more complex and complicated than I thought or knew from my friendship with her.

"The truth is she was a bit much for me," Oscar went on. "I liked a quieter life, and a more moral one. We didn't get caught, but I felt terribly guilty about what we'd done. She broke things off shortly after that. Still, I never forgot her. She was one-of-a-kind." He smiled.

"I agree. She and I were close. I found her." I choked up. As many times as I'd told the story, it didn't get any easier.

"I'm terribly sorry, my dear."

"I'm trying to figure out who might have wanted to harm her. Do you have any ideas?"

He shook his head. "I wish I did."

"Do you know if anyone else she dated is still around? Maybe they could help."

"I was mighty jealous of a fellow named Christopher Vermont. Have no idea where he might have ended up, including a box in the ground. But I suppose we were two out of dozens of relationships." He looked wistful.

This, again, gelled with what Stanley had said. "Thank you, Oscar. For both the information and for the muffin."

"My pleasure. Perhaps we'll meet again someday."

I nodded, grabbed my coffee and muffin, and said good-bye.

On the way home, I reflected on the information Oscar had provided. Could the break-in at the governor's office have anything to do with Trudy's murder? According to Oscar, they'd vandalized the office decades ago, so it was unlikely related to her death. But I'd been given a lead—Christopher Vermont, another of Trudy's beaus.

WHEN I HAD A CHANCE, I researched on the internet. The only likely Christopher Vermont, in terms of age and geography, had been dead for ten years. I assumed that meant I could count him out. It was a literal dead-end. Unless he'd come back to life and strangled Trudy. I giggled a little, imagining a zombie entering Trudy's house. Of course, it wasn't funny at all.

JASON ARRIVED THAT EVENING FOR his birthday surprise after the dinner rush had died down. I led him to the dining room table and told him to keep his eyes closed. I brought in the cake on one of my big platters.

"Okay, you can open your eyes now."

Jason's mouth dropped open. "This looks like a crab."

"Yep. It's a crab cake. Ha, ha."

"And it's red velvet?"

I nodded.

"How did you make the claws?" he asked.

"Fondant."

"This is so great, Kayla. Thank you. I love it. You're pretty fantastic, you know that?"

"So are you."

He got up, put his arms around me, and kissed me.

I cut us generous pieces and put them on dessert plates. We went over to the couch to eat.

"Extremely good," Jason said after taking a huge bite. "Have you considered offering the crab cake for sale?"

"I could. It's not perishable. I used vanilla frosting instead of cream cheese."

Sugar and Flour came into the room. They jumped up next to me and leaned in, eager to partake.

"Can they have a taste?" Jason asked.

"No. Chocolate is toxic to cats."

"Poor things. Never getting to have chocolate."

I found a couple of catnip mice in the depths of the couch and gave one to each cat.

"I'm very glad you were born, Jason," I said.

"I am, too, because thirty-seven years later, I'm here with you."

"Awww."

We tried to kiss, but Flour and Sugar abandoned their mice and sat between us. Then they meowed at Jason until he yielded the couch and had to go sit in the easy chair.

"I'm sorry," I said. "They're apparently possessive of me."

"We'll have to see about that. Because I will be seeing a lot more of you. If you're willing, that is."

"Oh, I am definitely willing."

Jason left a half hour later and we finally shared a kiss outside by his car. He promised to call the next day and drove off.

BACK INSIDE, I FOUND SOME MINIATURE CANDY CANES left over from the pie I'd made for Laura Fremont. I brought one over to the couch to munch on while I watched the news. Sugar and Flour hopped up next to me, sniffed at the candy, and jumped back down.

"Oh right. Some cats don't like peppermint. I totally respect that."

The news started. I was dismayed to learn that the police had yet to get a break in Trudy's murder case. Looked like my investigating would be ongoing.

THE NEXT AFTERNOON, I FOUND MY LOGIC GRID and looked it over. Unfortunately, I didn't have anything new to add. I doubted Oscar had killed Trudy. He may have been upset she'd broken up with him, but that had been decades ago. The only lead he'd come up with was another of Trudy's exes, who was dead.

Trudy's murder and my inability to determine whodunit hung over me like a big fat storm cloud. Truth be told, I liked storm clouds and wouldn't have minded pouring rain at the moment. I decided to go for a walk to clear my head and see if there was any sign of a gathering storm.

The day was sunny and not at all chilly. No signs of a storm, but the mild weather made for an enjoyable walk. As much as I liked rain, I didn't particularly want to be out in it.

Whether consciously or not, I ended up on Trudy's street. I girded myself for the sight of her house. Other than the brief glimpse of it when I'd picked up Sugar from Eileen, I hadn't been back. I knew I'd find myself experiencing a wave of grief and loss.

What I *didn't* expect to find was Jason trying to break in.

I APPROACHED AND RETREATED, THEN DID IT all over again. There was no doubt about it; Jason was outside Trudy's house, looking around as though he were trying to find a way in. My heart sank all the way to my feet. Jason? What was he doing here? He'd never said he'd known Trudy. Of course, he hadn't said he *hadn't* known her either. That was weird, right? Since, for obvious reasons, she'd been a topic of conversation from the time we'd met, he should have said one way or the other.

Should I call Brian? But what if Jason had a good reason to snoop around Trudy's house? Maybe he was looking at her flowers. He might be thinking of planting some of the same varieties. Yeah, that was probably it. He had been on his way to see me and he'd stopped to get a better look at Trudy's flowers. Of course, if he were coming to see me, Trudy's house was significantly out of his way. Plus, he'd told me he lived in an apartment with no balcony, patio, or garden, which pretty well shot that theory down. Besides, he was looking at the doors and windows and not the flowers at all.

Confrontation was beyond excruciating for me. Raised voices and disagreement became overstimulating in very little time. I knew I should talk to Jason but I couldn't. Not yet. I left for the clubhouse restaurant to see Isabella.

I STUMBLED TO A TABLE NEAR THE WATER and slumped into a chair. I cradled my head in my hands.

Isabella came over. "Kayla? What's going on? Are you okay?"

I looked up. "Not really. But before I tell you why, I want the biggest slice of cake you can give me without getting in trouble with Vincent, and a mocha with a tower of whipped cream."

"You must be bad off. You never order our cake. You say it's dry and bland."

"I'm desperate. I don't have any at home at the moment. I made Jason take home both his practice birthday cake and the finished product. And I don't feel like baking."

"Okay, now I know there's a big problem. You've never said you don't feel like baking. Baking is your go-to when you don't feel well." She sank into the seat next to me.

"Make the mocha caffeinated too."

"Are you sure about that?"

"Yes."

"You *are* bad off. What the heck is going on?"

I'd been planning to tell Isabella what I'd seen after fortifying myself. But I blurted out: "I saw Jason outside of Trudy's house."

"Doing what?"

"That, my friend, is the question. I have no idea. It looked like he was trying to break in."

"What? Why would he break in? Did you ask him what he was doing?"

"No. I snuck off and came here."

"You need to talk to him," she said. "Communication is the most important part of a relationship."

"What if he killed her?" I whispered. "Maybe he left something incriminating behind and he was trying to get it."

Ignoring Vincent's look from across the room, Isabella stayed put. "Sweetie, Jason did *not* murder Trudy."

"How do you know? I don't want to be blindsided."

"Let's think about it logically. What would the motive be?"

"I don't know."

"Exactly. There is no motive. Therefore, he didn't do it."

"What if you're wrong? He asked me out. What if he knows I'm looking into the murder and wants to keep close so he can keep track of what I discover? How serendipitous for him that he'd just met me."

Isabella raised her eyebrows. "I honestly don't think so. How would he have found out you're investigating? He doesn't live in Seaside Shores, does he?"

I shook my head. "No. His sister does, though."

"But had you even started investigating when he asked you out?"

I thought about it and told her no.

"He didn't do it, hon."

"Then what was he doing at Trudy's house today?" I moaned.

"There's only one way to get the answer to that. Ask him."

"Okay, but I want the cake and mocha. Caffeinated. I need fortifying."

"On the way. If you can't sleep tonight, don't blame me." She got up and went to fulfill my order.

I LINGERED OVER MY CAKE, WHICH WAS as chalky and flavorless as I remembered. Attempting to liven it up, I poured some coffee on top, to no avail. I would have to think about how to approach Vincent and convince him to order from me.

When I'd finished every crumb and drunk every molecule of coffee, I stared out at the ocean. A few children and their parents were braving the cold water by wading out into it. I shivered in solidarity. Even at its warmest, the water off of Oceanville never exceeded the mid-sixties.

But I couldn't sit here all day thinking about the water temperature. I had to face Jason. I wanted to know the truth, even if it was bad. I pushed my dirty dish and cup away from me, pulled money from my wallet and placed it on the table, and waved to Isabella on my way out. She gave me a look which I took to mean I was supposed to go fix this problem. I nodded at her to let her know that's exactly what I was doing.

I walked down to the wharf, trying to ignore the way my hands were shaking a little from the caffeine I wasn't accustomed to. I'd forgotten my clip-on sunglasses, and the bright sun shone in my face. Great. Caffeine and too much brightness. I was rapidly becoming overstimulated.

Jason grinned when he saw me, and my heart melted. Surely there was a rational explanation for why he was at Trudy's. He came over and gave me a quick hug. I couldn't help returning the embrace.

"This is a nice surprise," he said. "What can I get you?"

I'd just eaten a big piece of cake, which, while awful, counted as food. But instead of "Nothing, thank you," what came out of my mouth was, "How about a slice of one of my apple pies?"

"Coffee?"

I thought of the mocha I'd downed and decided decaf might be okay. "Sure. A decaf latte? Vanilla, please."

Once Jason had retrieved my order and we were seated in a booth, I looked into his ocean-blue eyes. I didn't know how to begin.

"What is it? Did something new happen?" he asked, concern all over his face. "Are you okay?"

"I saw you at Trudy's."

His face crumpled. "Oh," he said. He looked down at the table and wouldn't meet my eyes.

A big ball of pain filled my stomach. I stared at him, waiting for him to explain. He said nothing. I gathered my things, leaving my pie and coffee untouched.

"Kayla," he finally said.

"I have to go."

I went home, sank into the softness of the couch, and tried not to think about what my new boyfriend was hiding from me.

CHAPTER 7

THE NEXT MORNING, I BENT TO SUGAR AND FLOUR as they lay on the floor. I scratched their ears and chins, happy they were exactly who they seemed. No secrets here. When they went into the dining room to check their food bowls, I put on shoes and grabbed my phone and credit card, then stepped outside for a walk. I made my way to the coastal path and inhaled the sea air. A bitter wind blew in from the water, so I switched my plans to getting coffee. I headed for the clubhouse restaurant.

Isabella brought my coffee but didn't sit down. "I already had my fifteen-minute break, and Vincent will be on my case if I sit. Despite the fact that you're the only customer. Just tell me, what did Jason say when you talked to him?"

"He had no explanation. I know I should have pressed him, but I was exhausted. I went home instead."

"I'm sure he had nothing to do with the murder. Talk to him. Make up. I want to have a double date for the holiday party."

Recognition dawned. "Oh, so it really just comes back to you, then?"

"Doesn't everything?"

We grinned at each other, and I felt a little better. And more confident it would all work out okay.

"All right, I'm going," I said. "Right now. Can I have my coffee to go?"

I marched myself down to Fishes Do Come True and took a table. When Jason saw me, he shuffled over. I almost giggled at the hangdog look on his face and then remembered there was a chance, however slight, that he was a killer.

"I'm glad you're here," Jason said. "Are you going to let me explain?" He sat in the chair across from me.

Steeling myself, I leaned forward and said, "Yes, but it better be a good story and one that doesn't involve you hurting Trudy."

He threw his hands up in the air. "Kayla! I understand that we don't know each other that well yet. From what you do know, do you honestly think I'm capable of harming her?"

I said in a small voice, "No. I don't think so. But a tiny part of me was afraid it could be true. Jason, what were you doing there?"

"Okay. Here's the truth. The entire truth."

I sank back into my chair and wrapped my hands around my to-go cup.

Jason ran a hand through his dark hair. He looked into my eyes. "Leon Haskell is—was—one of Trudy's neighbors."

"Wait, I know that name. Isn't he the owner of Scales and Fins Restaurant?"

"Exactly. And he lives close to Trudy's house. Across the street."

"Okay..."

"Leon and I have a rocky history. One day, he and I got into it in his front yard. We were yelling and screaming, the whole nine yards. Trudy took a picture of me on the verge of slugging him. I was afraid someone would be coming to clean out her house and they'd find the photo."

I kept waiting for him to add something to the story.

"That's it?" I asked.

"No, that's not all. A couple of weeks before her death, Trudy sent me a letter telling me she took the picture and saying she wanted money. The guy seems great, right? He's involved in a last wishes charity. He hires felons. He donates his leftover food to homeless shelters. The truth is he's not a good person at all. But it would look like I was beating up on the Angel of Oceanville if the picture got out. It could have been bad for me and for the restaurant."

I stared at him for a number of seconds. Trudy blackmailed him? On the one hand, I couldn't believe it. And, yet, given all the revelations of the past few weeks, I was beginning to get a much different picture of the person Trudy was versus who I believed her to be.

"I didn't realize you even knew her," I said.

"I catered an event at the senior center a few years ago and met her. We chatted for a while. I liked her."

"Did you give her the money?"

"No, and nothing ever happened. She didn't release the picture. But if someone saw it and found out she blackmailed me, I'd be an obvious suspect."

"Did you hurt Leon?" I asked.

"The picture shows me about to take a punch. I stopped myself in time. I didn't hit him."

"You were actually going to break into her house to recover the picture?"

"Yes and no. I was seeing if a door or window was open. If so, it wouldn't technically be a break-in. As it happened, everything was locked up and I left." He looked sheepish.

"What if someone had seen you and called the police? They would have found it suspicious. They might have thought you were the killer, like I did for a minute and a half. At the very least, you might have been arrested."

"I know. It was incredibly stupid."

"I just wish you had talked to me about this."

"I didn't want you to think I go around beating people up. I don't, truly. But I screwed everything up by not telling you. Every time you talked about Trudy, I realized how much she meant to you and I should have come clean and told you. I'm sorry. Will you forgive me?"

I got up, leaned over to his chair, and hugged him. "Thank goodness I know what happened now. Of course I forgive you. We need to be honest with each other if this is going to work."

"I agree. Anything you'd like to tell me?"

"No. Nothing." My stomach knotted. I'd never told him I was investigating Trudy's murder.

"WHY WOULD TRUDY DO THAT? BLACKMAIL JASON?" I asked Isabella the next day as I helped her decorate the restaurant's Christmas tree. With Vincent away running errands, and the restaurant closed in advance of a private event, we were playing carols over the sound system. I'd already asked Isabella to turn the volume down, but the music was still too loud for me.

Isabella sang along to the carol currently playing, "We wish you a Merry Christmas . . ." She wasn't a bad singer, but she was no virtuosa.

"Iz, could you please stop singing and focus on what I'm asking you?"

"I don't know, hon. I guess she needed the money."

Isabella placed tinsel on the lower part of the tree. A lot. I took it off and she put it back on. Then we did the same thing twice more as though we were channeling Lucy and Ethel.

"She needed the money?" I repeated. "I guess that could be the reason. That's why she cheated at bingo, however that's possible. I wish she had told me instead of turning to a life of crime. I could have loaned her some. The business has been doing well lately. She told me once she had money from her family, but it could have dried up."

"I don't know the answer to that. Did her attorney say anything?"

"He only said that the proceeds from the sale of her house will go to animal shelters around the county. He didn't mention any other money."

"So it does sound as though she had run out," Isabella said.

"But cheating and blackmailing? I can't believe she would do that."

"I know. I'm really sorry, hon."

She started singing along to the music again, this time to "Deck the Halls." I needed to keep her talking.

"I almost forgot to tell you," I said. "I met up with Oscar Lancaster, Cynthia Amandoli's father, at the Otter Café. He dated Trudy back in the early eighties."

"Did he have any information?"

"He told me he and Trudy broke into the governor's office when they were together and committed some vandalism. More bad news about Trudy. It just keeps coming."

"Oh no. Did he tell you anything else?"

I shook my head. "He didn't have any idea who could have hurt her."

Isabella launched into the next verse of "Deck the Halls."

The tree looked nice, if heavy on tinsel. "Iz, I think I need to get home. I'm exhausted."

"Okay. Go get some rest. Talk to you soon."

I trudged back home, not even looking at my beloved ocean on the way. I was in a funk. Jason was so gentle. I never would have guessed he would come close to slugging someone. And Trudy engaging in blackmail? What next?

I was keeping my own secret by not telling Jason I was investigating Trudy's murder. Would he think I was putting myself in danger? Probably, and he might ask me to stop. I wasn't going to, but he had the right to know. I unlocked the front door of the cottage and went inside, my conscience nagging at me. Before I let myself get too comfortable, I left again.

I walked down to the wharf once again and sat smack in the middle of the restaurant so Jason would be sure to see me.

He came over and asked if I wanted to order something.

"Chowder in a bread bowl. But before you go, Jason, I have to tell you something."

"Okay. Shoot."

I took a deep breath. "I have been investigating Trudy's murder. By talking to people and trying to gather clues."

He looked back at me, not speaking.

Unnerved by his reaction, I said, "I'm sorry I didn't tell you. I should have."

"Kayla, come with me." He took me out to the deck and sat me down at a table. Each time I tried to speak, he put up a finger to stop me. He went back and forth to the kitchen, returning with chowder in a bread bowl and a salad for each of us. He left once more and came back with a jacket, which he draped across my shoulders.

"Okay. Let's eat," he said as he sat across from me.

"Wait, wait, wait. Aren't you upset with me?"

"Kayla, the fact that you are looking into Trudy's murder doesn't surprise me. I already suspected based on a few things you've said."

"Really?"

"Yes." He didn't seem at all perturbed.

"Aren't you worried I'll get hurt . . . or even killed?"

"Eat some of the bread bowl. I baked it just before you came in. Dip it in the chowder. Yes, of course I'm concerned. But I know Trudy was like a grandmother to you. I doubt anything I say will stop you. Am I right?"

"Yes. You're right."

"I care about you. And I hope, on a stack of your delicious chocolate cakes, that you are careful about it, and if anything gets too dicey, you'll go straight to the police. I'm not going to tell you what to do or not do."

I leapt up and went over to his side of the table to hug him.

"You're terrific," I told him.

"It's nice to know you feel that way." He smiled at me. "I do appreciate that you came all the way down here to confess. You're a little on the late side but I'll take it."

I crossed my eyes at him.

"Walk on the beach after we finish?" he asked.

"Rain check? I'm tired."

"Of course."

After lunch, we said good-bye and I left for home, thinking how nice it was that Jason understood when I became fatigued and didn't take it personally. He was the perfect boyfriend for me.

AT HOME, DESPITE THE FACT THAT JASON AND I WERE FINE—he wasn't a killer and we had no secrets between us—a deep sadness settled over me. I was seeing another side of Trudy that was someone I didn't know and wasn't very nice either. Cheating at bingo and blackmailing people—even if they didn't pay—were not victimless crimes. Look at what happened to Jason. He put himself in a situation that could have gotten him arrested.

I flopped onto my bed. Fortunately, I had two adorable balls of fur who sensed where I was, ran into the room, and hopped up next to me, immediately raising my spirits.

As I was scratching Flour's chin, my cell phone rang. I took the phone from my pocket and was glad to see it was Jason.

"Hey," I answered.

"Hey back at you. What with everything that's been going on, I forgot to ask you to Thanksgiving at the restaurant tomorrow afternoon. What do you say?"

"I completely forgot it's Thanksgiving. Trudy and I were going to go to Sam's." I sighed heavily.

"I'm sorry, Kayla. Will you take me and my restaurant as your second choice?"

"Of course I will. What time should I be there?"

"Around two. I'll try to sit with you for part of it, but I can't promise I'll be able to stay the whole time."

"That's okay. As long as we're in the same place at the same time, I'll be happy."

The thought that I'd have a nice meal the next day and be around Jason further improved my mood. I was ready to get into the kitchen to begin an order.

INSTEAD OF TURKEY AND THE USUAL FIXINGS, Jason served his "Clam and Crab Cornucopia" the next day. The dinner, which included a whole crab, clam chowder, salad, corn, rolls, and french fries, was fantastic.

Jason joined me for about half an hour at dessert, apple pie he'd ordered from Icings Bakery in town way before he met me.

I ate way too much, kissed Jason good-bye, and went home to take a nap.

THE NEXT DAY, ISABELLA AND I BRAVED THE FOG for a walk along the coastal path before work. My friend looked fit in stylish athletic wear. As we began walking, she edged out in front of me as though we were in a road race. I asked her to slow down a bit.

"Do you believe that you can care for someone even if they did bad things?" I asked after a while.

"Are we talking white lies or murder?"

"Halfway between those two."

"Blackmail and cheating at bingo, you mean?"

"Right." I looked out at the ocean. A fishing boat went by with its lights on, barely visible through the fog.

"Sometimes people have understandable reasons for doing bad things," Isabella said. "Maybe she was embarrassed that she ran out of money and didn't know what else to do."

I looked at her for a long moment and nodded. She nodded back.

"I keep meaning to ask you," I said. "Do you know anything about an observatory Trudy had commissioned? She never told me about it."

"No, but it doesn't surprise me. She loved stargazing."

"I never knew that."

"She majored in astronomy in college."

"Really? How could I not know so many things about her? What a lousy friend I must have been."

"Oh, sweetie. It's okay. She knew you loved her, and she loved you back. I can't tell you how many times she raved about one of your cakes or pies to me. Or about you in general."

I brightened up. "Yeah?"

"Yeah."

We walked for forty-five minutes, and then Isabella left me to get ready for work. I headed for my cottage, wishing I'd known about Trudy's love for astronomy. There were a number of spots in Oceanville we could have visited to stargaze. Now we'd never be able to do that. I felt renewed resolve to find the person who had taken away her future. I had to figure out my next step.

I AWAKENED THE NEXT MORNING THINKING NOT about Trudy's murder, but rather the upcoming Christmas holiday, which was less than a month away. Now that I'd confirmed with my mom that I'd be visiting her and my stepfather in the San Francisco Bay Area, I had to shop for presents for them. And I wanted to buy gifts for Isabella and Jason too. I powered up my laptop to do some online shopping.

After taking care of presents for Jason, Isabella, and my stepdad, I turned my attention to my mom. She'd mentioned how chilly it had been on her daily walks lately. Easy enough. I ordered some cute mittens and a pair of fuzzy socks. I saw a beautiful yarn scarf and remembered I'd meant to knit one for her. In fact, Trudy and I had planned on knitting scarves together. A heaviness came over me, a common occurrence in the three weeks since Trudy had died. I sensed it would be a long time before the worst of the grief passed.

The cats came running right when I was ready to order a light-blue scarf that would look great with my mom's eyes. They leapt up next to me on the couch. Then they took turns walking across the laptop keyboard, minimizing and maximizing the screen and pressing keys at will.

I pushed the laptop away from them and gave in to their demands for attention.

JASON CALLED THAT AFTERNOON, AND AFTER we'd exchanged a few sweet nothings, he said, "This might not be the best time, but I have something to bring up. My sister would like to meet you. Is it too early for meeting the family?"

"Since you talked about the two of us meeting during our first date, no, I don't think it's too early."

"Great. How about a Christmas activity? A quiet, not-crowded one, of course."

"What would you think about driving through North Pole Place after dark?" I suggested. "The decorations are supposed to be incredible. The residents decorate right after Thanksgiving."

"North Pole Place?" Jason repeated.

"That's what we call the group of streets that go over-the-top with decorations."

"That sounds perfect. Paula loves that kind of stuff. We can have dessert at the restaurant after. Tomorrow night, if you're free?"

I agreed, and Jason said he'd pick me up at seven.

PAULA ANSWERED THE DOOR THE NEXT NIGHT tugging at the top of her pants.

"I should never have bought these," she said. "They're so uncomfortable." We all laughed.

"Why don't you change?" I said. "Don't be dressed up on my account."

"I like you, Kayla. I'll be right back. Come in."

Jason and I sat on the couch and waited for Paula. A black Lab arrived in the room, came up to us, and nuzzled our hands. Jason introduced her as Midnight. We gave her a few scratches.

Paula returned a few minutes later wearing a white sweatshirt and green velour sweatpants. She smiled at us, and her blue eyes, very much like Jason's, lit up. She'd bundled her hair, a few shades lighter than Jason's, into a high ponytail.

"That's much better," she said. "We've done this the wrong way around. Usually I get to know someone first before I take off my clothes. Hi, I'm Paula."

I got up and shook her hand. "Nice to meet you. I know exactly what you mean about pants. I can only wear jeans or sweatpants. Or corduroy if it's not too warm. Anything else I find uncomfortable. Frankly, there are even pajamas I can't stand if the fabric isn't right."

"Yep. I hear you."

"Are you ready to go, Sis?" Jason asked.

"Sure. I'm excited."

We piled into Jason's Honda Civic and drove to Seaview Lane to begin our tour of North Pole Place. The residents had tried to outdo each other with countless strings of red and green lights, inflatable reindeer and Santas, and oversized ornaments on the trees in their yards. There was a long line of cars moving through, but that was all right with us as it allowed plenty of time to absorb the sights.

We oohed and aahed as we caught sight of each new house and its decorations.

"Look at those inflatables, Kayla. Giant cupcakes," Jason said.

"Love them. Do you see the house across the street? Lobsters and crabs wearing Santa hats."

"Adorable," Paula said.

When we'd driven through all the streets in North Pole Place, we headed over to the wharf. Jason parked and the three of us climbed out.

Paula took my arm. "That was such fun. I'm so glad you're dating

Jason. He's a terrific guy who hasn't found the right woman yet. From what I hear, you're perfect for him."

"Right here. I'm standing right here," Jason said.

"Well, it's true," Paula said.

"You don't always have to say everything that comes into your head," Jason said, but he was smiling. The three of us walked up the wharf to Fishes Do Come True, our arms linked.

Over coffee and slices of one of my chocolate cakes, we talked about the foods, smells, and weather we found irksome. Even Jason had a few things to say. We all agreed he might be an HSP.

Once we'd covered the things that bothered us, we started sharing what affected us positively.

"The colors of the sunset. The sunrise, too, although I'm not always awake for it," I said.

"A perfectly done steak," Jason contributed.

I thought for a moment. "A painting that takes your breath away. Jason's clam chowder in a bread bowl." Jason grabbed my hand and squeezed it.

"There's nothing better than being inside, not too hot and not too cold," Paula said.

I added, "Cozy under a blanket with a good book and two cats snuggled against you."

"I heard about Flour and Sugar. They sound so cute," she said.

"You'll have to come over and meet them. I can't believe I ever lived my life without them."

"I'd love to."

Paula raved about the chocolate cake and asked if I'd make one for her birthday. Of course, I agreed. All in all, it was a successful evening.

After we dropped Paula off at her house, Jason took my hand and held it as we drove to my place. He said, "She likes you a lot."

"She probably likes all the girlfriends you introduce her to."

"All the girlfriends? There haven't been that many, and I can assure you she hasn't reacted to any of them as well as she reacted to you."

"I like her too."

"And I like you."

"I like you as well." I giggled. He pulled the car over to the side of the road and stopped my giggling with a long kiss. One of the great pleasures of life, kisses from Jason.

ON MONDAY, WHEN I CAME HOME from enjoying a decaf mocha at the clubhouse restaurant with Isabella, I found a tall package at my doorstep. Had someone sent me an early Christmas present? I took the package inside and kept it away from my curious cats.

At the coffee table, I tore the package open to find a stack of light-blue scarves. I counted. Twenty-two. Twenty-two light-blue scarves.

What the heck?

I pulled up my store account, and sure enough, I had ordered twenty-two of the pretty scarf I'd looked at for my mom. Plus, I'd asked for express delivery.

Except I *hadn't* ordered twenty-two scarves and asked for express delivery. I hadn't even ordered one scarf for my mom. I'd forgotten all about it. Had the cats done this when they were walking around on the keyboard? They must have.

The two were nestled together in the easy chair. I gave them the stink-eye.

Deciding I could work with this mistake, I started a list. My mom would get a scarf as she was the original recipient. My stepdad, Bob, could have one as well. He and my mom might look cute wearing the same scarf. They were already beginning to look alike the way long-term couples sometimes do. I remembered Stanley Young draping a blanket over himself when I'd first visited him and Beau. I could give him a scarf as a holiday present, and maybe in the process, succeed in extracting more information about Trudy's past. Did dogs wear scarves? Could I give Beau one?

On the last day of November, I set aside the scarves that had already been earmarked for recipients and bundled the rest of them into my messenger bag. I headed out, prepared to distribute any and all as necessary. First, I gave one to Isabella at the clubhouse restaurant. She put it on while Vincent glared at her and looked pointedly at his watch. I went over to him and handed him a scarf. When he accepted it, I decided to press my advantage.

"Have you thought any more about ordering desserts from me?" I asked.

Vincent glanced at Isabella, who smiled sweetly at him. "I haven't decided yet," he said before leaving for the kitchen.

That was better than an outright no. On the way out, I passed Isabella's neighbors, Donald and Mary Cohen, who were waiting for a takeout order. I double backed and gave each a scarf. They thanked me profusely.

I ran into Vicky and her daughter Angie on the coastal path. They both got scarves.

"Thank you, Kayla," Vicky said. "It's lovely."

Angie ran her scarf across her face. "It's so soft." She let out a happy yelp and ran off to look at an otter bobbing in the water.

Vicky smiled at me and said, "Kayla, I can't thank you enough for turning us onto the HSP thing. Angie is much happier. No more tights or shirts with the tags in them. She's even letting me get the tangles out of her hair because I'm gentler. She's doing great."

"That's wonderful. I'm so glad you're aware of it now, while she's still young. It's a relatively new discovery for me. I could have been spared a lot of discomfort if I'd known about it earlier. It's taken me a while to get my life the way I want it to be."

"I've been reading the books you recommended," Vicky said. "It's interesting that even animals can be highly sensitive."

"Yes, and in the same percentage as humans. Fifteen to twenty percent of the population. My cats definitely *aren't* HSPs, however."

"I wonder if our cat might be," Vicky said. "She gets anxious, especially with noises. She hides under the bed a lot."

"Could be."

"We better get going. Nice to see you, Kayla. Come on, honey, we have to go."

Angie skipped back to us. She reached up to hug me and I hugged her back. She was quite a sweetheart. I said good-bye and told them I'd see them soon.

Before going home, I stopped at Tristan's to give him a scarf. When I said the scarf looked great with his blue-framed glasses, he immediately left to look at himself in a mirror. On his return, he seemed pleased with himself, and lest I receive an earful of how wonderful he was, I told him I had to go.

With a number of scarves left, I decided to donate the extras to a homeless shelter. I got on the computer to look up some addresses and saw I had an email from Vicky.

Hi Kayla,

It was great to see you today. Thank you so much for the scarves and again for the information on HSPs. I can't believe how much it resonates.

I'm so grateful because I feel I can now give Angie what she needs. She's less stressed than usual, happier than ever.

She's turning eight on Saturday and we're having an otter-themed party. If it's not too late, we'd like to commission her cake from you. I was going to pick up something at the supermarket (!), but if you're available, could you draw up a couple of designs and we'll decide? She loves anything chocolate. She'd also like you to come to the party. Say you'll come.

Best,
Vicky

I wrote back right away with a few ideas for the cake and accepted the invitation. I found a homeless shelter for the scarves and left for the mini-van to deliver them.

BACK AT HOME, IT WAS TIME TO RETURN TO SLEUTHING. I picked up my logic grid and wondered what to do next.

I had a question mark next to "bingo." Burton Engel's assertion that Trudy cheated at bingo had been nagging at me. How was that possible? The numbers were called and you either had them in a neat little row on your card or you didn't. I believed Burton's alibi—though it sported a question mark as it remained unverified—but had other bingo players resented Trudy's success and wanted to get rid of her? Burton had told me bingo could pay a pretty penny. I put aside the conundrum that Trudy's cash hadn't been taken. Perhaps the killer had been scared away before he could steal the money.

Returning to the senior center the next morning, I found the woman who'd sold me my bingo card the day I'd met Burton. I introduced myself.

"Molly Tremaine," she said, shaking my hand. "I remember you." Today, Molly wore her red hair in a braided ponytail positioned over her shoulder.

"Molly, I don't really know how to say this, but is it possible for someone to cheat at bingo?"

She blinked a couple of times and didn't answer.

"Someone suggested it," I said. "Trudy Dillingham was winning an awful lot, and this person didn't believe it was on the up and up."

"No, there's no way to cheat. We put the balls in the cage and they're picked at random, then announced and shown to the room." Molly straightened the sleeves of her green blouse. "Anyone who calls bingo has to go up to the caller and get their win verified. It's impossible to get around that." She paused. "Well, unless . . ."

"Unless what?"

"I suppose if . . ."

"Yes?"

"If the caller was an accomplice. So, let's say Trudy calls bingo quickly, before anyone else can. She goes up to the caller and the caller confirms she won. I'm not saying that happened, but you could talk to Doris Walters. She's been calling the numbers for years." Molly bit her lip and fiddled with the multiple bracelets on her wrist.

"Thank you."

"Kayla, may I trust you to be discreet if you find it to be true? It's something we'll have to attend to, of course, but I'd rather keep it quiet while we work out what to do."

"Of course."

"I appreciate it."

"Do you know where I could find Doris?" I asked. "I'd prefer to talk to her alone, not while bingo is going on."

Molly checked her watch. "She likes to stop by the clubhouse for coffee around nine and go down to the beach afterward. She's probably at the beach now."

I followed the coastal path from the senior center to the clubhouse. Once I'd climbed down the steps to the beach, I spotted a sixty-something woman with long, curly white hair standing in the wet sand at the shore. I recognized her as the bingo caller from the day I'd talked to Burton.

I removed my shoes so I could walk toward her, but stopped in my tracks when I realized she was tossing food to the seagulls. I didn't like birds in general and gulls in particular. A few customers at Fishes Do Come True had had food stolen right off their forks by determined gulls. I hadn't asked Jason yet if we could eat inside from now on, but I was considering it.

I approached Doris and the gulls with caution.

"Doris?" I called.

She turned, and at that second a gull swooped down to her and swiped the food from her hand. She shrieked. Then she laughed. My heart pounded just witnessing the scene. She, on the other hand, appeared delighted by the experience.

"I'm Doris, yes," she said.

I walked a little closer to her. "I'm Kayla Jeffries. Are you . . . are you supposed to be doing that?"

"Technically, no. But I give them healthy things like seeds."

I nodded. To each their own, I supposed. "I wonder if I could talk to you about bingo." I paused, realizing I hadn't thought this through. What was I going to do, ask if she and Trudy colluded in a cheating scheme? I decided to circle around the subject.

"Trudy Dillingham played bingo a lot, I understand. I . . . found her."

Doris's face crumpled, followed by the rest of her, and she sank into the sand. I went over to her. The seagulls circled, and I looked up at them warily.

"I'm so sorry," I said. "You were close?"

She sniffed. "Yes. Who are you again?"

"Kayla Jeffries. I was a friend too. A good friend."

"It's simply unbelievable. I cannot come to terms with the fact that she's shuffled off this mortal coil."

She was certainly colorful. I sank down beside her and winced when my bottom hit wet sand. "I know."

We were silent as we gazed out at the ocean. The gulls, sensing no more food was forthcoming, had dispersed. Wave after wave rolled toward the shore, a hypnotic sight.

Doris said, "We had this thing going, Trudy and I. She'd say she had bingo when she didn't, bring her card up, and I'd say she'd won. We didn't do it every round. That would have been suspicious. But enough for us to both have some nice pocket money."

I couldn't believe it had been that easy. She'd confessed to me.

"Did anyone suspect?" I asked.

"Don't know. They wouldn't have been able to prove it. I took care to throw away Trudy's cards. Oh, I miss her so much."

I patted her back. I wondered if she had converted someone new to the scam. Burton, perhaps? That would ensure a number of wins for him.

"I could never do it with anyone else," Doris said.

That answered *that* question.

"Do you happen to know why Trudy left early the afternoon she died?" I asked.

"It was odd that she left. I'd seen her around two thirty, and we talked about bingo starting earlier because of everything being shuffled around for a private party. I didn't see her again. We never had a chance to win any games."

"Win" was a strong word considering the scheme they'd concocted.

Doris got to her feet, turned around, and did a downward dog yoga pose, impressing me with her flexibility.

"If you're looking for a suspect, she'd been having a spat with her gardener," she said.

"Her gardener?" What could possibly irritate a gardener so much that he'd kill a client?

"Yes. They had some disagreement about the pot."

"What kind of disagreement could they have had about a pot?"

Doris laughed. "Not *a* pot. *Pot.* You know. Marijuana."

"Trudy had marijuana plants?"

She exited from the pose. "Yes. She imbibed once in a while, but mostly she gave it out to folks at the center for medicinal purposes."

Could I take one more revelation about Trudy? Marijuana was now legal in California, but once again, I couldn't square this Trudy with the woman I knew.

"Do you know the gardener's name?" I asked.

"Hmm. I don't recall. I think it starts with a *C*."

A gull made its way toward Doris and she reached into her pocket for more seeds. When a few others joined, I took it as my cue to leave. I made a mental note to decide whether to disclose Doris's revelations to Molly. I liked Doris and didn't want her arrested, but Molly and the senior center probably had the right to know that several of their bingo games had been compromised. On the other hand, Trudy was dead and Doris didn't plan to continue the cheating. I decided to get Jason's take.

I bid good-bye to Doris and walked through the sand to the steps. Sitting on a stair, I brushed sand off my feet and put on my shoes. Up at the clubhouse, I saw Isabella through one of the restaurant windows bringing a cup of coffee to a customer. She looked busy, so I joined the coastal walk and went down to the wharf to pay Jason an impromptu visit.

We had hot cocoa and shared a piece of one of my apple pies. I relayed the conversation I'd had with Doris and presented my quandary over reporting what I'd learned.

"Maybe I should let sleeping dogs lie," I said.

Jason nodded. "I think that's the best plan."

Meanwhile, I had a new lead—Trudy's gardener. I wanted to follow up as soon as possible, so I gave Jason a kiss and left.

CHAPTER 8

A T HOME, I MADE MYSELF A SANDWICH and wondered how I could talk to Trudy's gardener to find out more about the "spat" he'd had with her. How to find him? I wracked my brain, but couldn't recall Trudy ever mentioning her gardener, let alone giving me his name. I set out for the Seaside Shores offices, where I told the receptionist, Miranda, that I was interested in a gardener. She gave me Cole London's name.

"He maintains the communal spaces. Grass, trees, flower beds, that kind of thing."

"Do you know how I could get ahold of him? I'd like to get him booked. I'm having a Christmas party and the yard is a mess." I wasn't having a Christmas party and I didn't have a yard, but it was a way to get Cole's phone number.

Miranda made a number of fast keystrokes on her computer. "He's at Alden Park right now."

"Thanks."

I walked over to the park, which was in the same block of Otter Street as the community offices. A sign at the entrance informed me that the park had been named after Theresa Alden, the founder of Seaside Shores. Just past the sign was a botanical garden with California native plants and flowers. I strolled through the garden, admired a dolphin fountain, and passed a kids' playground.

Eventually, I found a gardener planting bulbs in a newly-fertilized flower bed. I tapped him on the back.

"Cole?"

He turned around and looked up at me.

"Can I talk to you for a second? I'm Kayla Jeffries, a resident here."

He stood, took off his gardening gloves, and nodded.

"I found Trudy after she was . . . murdered. I'm trying to figure out why someone would do that to her. Can you tell me if she was growing weed?"

His forehead crinkled. "Trudy?"

"I thought she was a client of yours. Trudy Dillingham? An older lady?"

"Sorry. No idea what you're talking about. Must be another guy. Cliff Reed does a lot of the gardening for the residents' yards. You might try him."

"Any idea how I could get in touch with him?"

"He lives here. You can look him up in the directory."

"Thank you." I left, feeling that detective work was a lot of following one lead only to be given another. Cliff could wait until tomorrow.

I WENT HOME AND BAKED a few dozen Christmas sugar cookies. I made a large cup of cocoa and ate several of the cookies, which I'd designed in shapes of trees, reindeer, and presents. They were good, and I felt a lot better afterward. I put away the leftovers and cleaned the kitchen.

THE NEXT MORNING, I LOOKED UP CLIFF REED in the Seaside Shores directory. I gave him a call, saying I was interested in hiring him but would like to meet first. He told me he'd be working at Jan Williams's house for the day, so I arranged to meet him there.

Fortunately, Jan didn't have an issue with me coming to her door and asking to speak with her gardener. She didn't even ask me why.

That was the good news. The bad news was I found Cliff blasting a leaf blower on the patio. My nervous system was particularly affected by noise and this was noise on steroids. I asked him to turn it off. He didn't hear me. Because he kept moving around, I had to chase after him. At last I reached him and touched his elbow. When he looked back at me, I motioned to him to turn the blower off.

He switched off the blower, removed his earplugs, and turned around to face me. I was so relieved that the blower was off that my shoulders relaxed and I let out a long breath I didn't know I was holding.

"Thank you. I'm hypersensitive to noise."

"Sounds painful," he said. "Do you have a shrink for that?"

I decided to answer him. "First of all, there's nothing wrong with getting help when it's needed. But being an HSP—highly sensitive person—isn't a mental illness. It's a trait, like green eyes or freckles. We have strong reactions to internal and external stimuli, like noise. Okay?"

"Okay, okay. Don't get your panties in a twist," he responded. "Who are you, anyway?"

"I'm Kayla. We spoke on the phone earlier?"

"Right. I've gotta tell you, though. I'm booked for two months out."

That worked for me. After this encounter, I was never going to hire him, even if I *had* a yard.

"That's okay," I said. "I have something else to talk to you about. I found Trudy Dillingham after she was killed. She was a client of yours, I think? Can you tell me if she was growing pot?"

Cliff sighed as he walked over to a flower bed, knelt down, and pulled some weeds. I followed.

"Cliff?" I prompted.

With his back to me, he said, "She was."

"Did you have some kind of disagreement about it?"

A few beats went by before he said, "Yeah. She promised to cut me in."

"Cut you in? On what?"

He glanced backward at me briefly and then returned to his weeding. "The sales."

"I . . . I thought she was giving it away?"

He stopped weeding, stood, and turned to me. "No way. She was charging a lot. Quality pot isn't that easy to grow but I gave it the right care. Not once did she give me any money from her sales."

If Cliff had come to Trudy's door, she would have answered since he was her gardener. He worked with his hands and easily could have strangled her. What now? Was I in danger? I decided I wasn't, with Jan close by.

"Look, I gotta keep moving, okay?" he said. "I'm sorry she's dead. Sure, she could have cut me in, but otherwise, she was a nice lady."

"One last question. Where were you the afternoon she died? November fourth?"

"I was working. I have a wife and a family to support. Some of us have jobs. Unlike others of us who can interrogate people in the middle of the day."

He returned to the leaf blower and I went inside. Jan sat at the kitchen table drinking coffee.

"Get what you need?" she asked.

"I'm not sure. Do you have him over regularly?"

"Every Thursday."

"Was he here the day of Trudy's murder? November the fourth?"

"There was a day he called in sick. Let me look at the calendar."

She walked over to a little desk area at the end of the kitchen counter. She put on reading glasses, wet her finger, and flipped backward through a calendar. "Yeah. Same day. Wait, you don't think . . ." Whether consciously or not, Jan put a hand to her throat.

"Oh, I'm sure he didn't," I said, not at all sure. "I'm only trying to eliminate people who had contact with her."

"Right, right." Despite her words, Jan looked worried.

"Is Austin going to be home soon?"

"Yeah, he's due any minute."

"Good. I'm sure everything's fine, but I'll stay until he gets here."

Austin came home shortly, and I left, remembering to check what kind of vehicle Cliff had arrived in. A white truck with DOUBLE, DOUBLE, SOIL AND TROUBLE on the side was parked across the street from the Williams's house. As I expected, he hadn't driven over in his personal car, but I gave him points for the Shakespearean business name.

I talked to Jason on the phone later and told him about my meeting with Cliff.

"I guess it could have been him, but why didn't he take the wad of cash in her dresser?" I said. "If he wanted a cut from the pot sales, there was money right there. In fact, that's a problem with Trudy's fellow bingo players too. The killer didn't take any money."

"They could have been scared away before they had a chance to take it."

"Why kill her first, then? If someone wanted money, they could have taken it and left her alone."

"I don't know, honey."

"Cliff lied. He told me he was working the day Trudy died, but Jan said he called in sick. I have to find out where he was."

"Be careful," Jason said. "I want you to be safe."

We said good-bye and hung up. I shut myself in the kitchen. I now had two pending projects: the raspberry cake for the wedding couple who'd delegated the flavor and design choices to me, and Angie's birthday dessert. I'd deliver the raspberry cake the next day for the evening wedding.

Saturday morning, with Angie's cake secure in a blue box, I stopped by Stanley's house on the way to the party. This time, he didn't answer at all. I dug into my messenger bag for a notepad and pen, wrote a quick note, placed it on top of two scarves, and left everything on the doormat. Frustrated that I hadn't made contact with Stanley, I put it behind me for now and walked over to Wave Street to Vicky and Angie's house.

I was surprised to see Tristan sitting cross-legged on the grass in the front yard, leading Angie and four other girls in what looked to be an art project. He waved at me and I smiled back.

Angie ran over to me. She wore a blue tulle skirt without tights, and a tee shirt with an otter on it. She was much more comfortable than when we'd met for the first time.

"Hi, sweetheart. Happy birthday."

"Thank you. I'm having a really good party. Can I see the cake?"

"Of course. Let's go into the kitchen and I'll show you."

Both Vicky and Angie were delighted with the design on the chocolate sheet cake. One half featured a sandy beach with a fondant Angie lying on a chaise; the other half, a bright-blue ocean with an otter on his back holding an abalone in his paws.

"Oh my gosh. Mom, isn't it the most beautiful thing you've ever seen?" Angie raved.

"You've outdone yourself, Kayla," Vicky said. "I hate to cut it. We'll have to take plenty of pictures beforehand, won't we, honey?"

Angie nodded.

"You better get back to your guests now."

"Will you come, too, Kayla?" Angie asked.

"Sure."

Angie and I went back outside and joined the art project.

I had a great time at the party, doing all the things I'd liked to do as a child. In addition to the craft, we hopscotched on the sidewalk, played a word game, and ate hot dogs and chips before the cake. After dessert, Angie opened her gifts. I'd bought her a string of fairy lights for her room and was gratified when she exclaimed over them. I had a similar string in my bedroom that I plugged in when I didn't want the bright overhead light on.

When everyone was saying good-bye and leaving, Tristan came up to me.

"Need a ride, doll?"

"No, thanks. I think I'll walk."

On the way home, I thought back to my childhood. My parents had told me I threw tantrums regularly and took a while to calm down. Now I knew I was probably reacting to being overstimulated in some way. I was glad Angie and her parents would have an easier time of it than we had.

At home, I started in on my desserts for the tree lighting party the next night. Soon I was in the baking zone and feeling good.

THAT EVENING, WHEN JASON AND I MET FOR DINNER at The Seashore Diner in downtown Oceanville, I handed over the light-blue scarf I'd set aside for him.

"Thank you. I've been wanting a blue scarf," he said, immediately winding it around his neck.

"It looks great with your eyes. Sugar and Flour have good taste." At his puzzled look, I told him the whole story of how the cats had jumped on the computer and placed the order. He laughed.

We ordered grilled cheese sandwiches and fries and chose a few songs from the table jukebox.

"What is it about baking that you love?" Jason asked as he held my hand across the table.

"So much. Trying out different flavor combinations is one of my favorite parts. It's fun even if I end up making mistakes. I love decorating. When it goes the way I want it to, I feel like I'm creating works of art."

"Like my crab cake."

"Yeah, that's a particular favorite of mine. I'm also fond of the cake I brought to the party today."

I showed him a picture on my phone and he agreed it was excellent work, making my heart swell.

"There's also something about mixing and kneading . . . it's relaxing," I said. "But I also like that it's precise. Or it should be. I like that I can control it, I suppose."

"Something you can control in a world that's out of control?" Jason had a smile on his face, but I detected sadness behind his eyes.

"Yes, like Trudy's murder," I said.

"I know her death has been hard on you, Kayla. I'm so sorry you've had to deal with it."

"It has been hard, yes. I'm also finding out so many things about her that I didn't know. I don't mean just the bad stuff. She majored in astronomy in college. I have no idea if she ever did anything with her degree. Did she work at all? I have no clue. It turns out I didn't know her well at all."

"I'm sure that's not true."

"Maybe not completely true. What about you? When you talked about the world being out of control a minute ago, I could tell there was something behind that. Do you want to talk about it?"

Jason broke eye contact and picked up the catsup bottle. He put it down again and returned my gaze. "When I was a kid, my parents divorced. I know your folks did too. This was at another level. The divorce was ugly. As an adult, I've shied away from serious relationships. There've been some short relationships and then a longer one. It didn't work out, but I was okay with that. I think I was relieved. I never want to get divorced. The only way to ensure that is not to get married. Probably the best thing of all is to not get too involved."

I felt a flutter in my stomach. I was nowhere near ready for a long-term commitment, but was he saying he didn't want to develop our relationship further? What did that mean?

"However . . ." He gave me a lopsided grin.

"Yes?"

"I find myself falling for you. I don't think I'm gonna be able to escape this one. I care about you, Kayla."

"I care about you too."

"I think we should take it slow. I like the girlfriend/boyfriend thing. Past that, I don't know."

"That's perfectly okay with me. Let's take it slow."

To prove our dedication, we leaned across the table and kissed—slowly.

"Hey, you two, get a room."

It was Isabella. She and Brian approached our booth. Brian, wearing jeans and a polo shirt, looked very different from when he was in work mode, and much more approachable. After I made the necessary introductions, we invited them to join us. I caught Isabella's eye and gestured to Brian, wondering if he knew she'd gone dancing with Jack, the newest resident of the community. She merely smiled.

We spent an enjoyable hour together, and Brian didn't once mention my needing to butt out of the murder investigation. Of course, maybe he thought I already had.

After the four of us split a slice of mud pie and parted ways, Jason and I decided to call it a night. I was tired after the long day. We got into Jason's car and drove to Seaside Shores.

Unfortunately, my day was about to get longer. We turned onto Sea Lion Drive to see a yellow Labrador in a blue scarf walking down the street by himself. It had to be Beau, Stanley Young's old dog.

I put my hand on Jason's arm. "It's Beau. I know him."

Jason swung over to the side of the road and we got out of the car.

"Come here, boy," Jason called to him. Beau padded over. We scratched his back and ears and he licked our hands.

"This can't be good," I said. "This is Stanley Young's dog. Stanley would never let Beau out of his sight."

"Let's take him home and find out what's going on."

Beau, agreeable if a tad arthritic, climbed into the backseat with Jason's help. I spoke soothingly to him as I directed Jason to Stanley's house. We parked and Jason cracked the windows.

We went up the front walkway and found the door wide open. Jason motioned to me to stay behind him. We stepped inside.

Stanley lay in an unnatural position on the living room floor, the scarf I'd left for him that morning wound tightly around his neck. I let out a gasp.

Jason and I dropped to the floor. I started chest compressions but Jason put his hand to my back. "It's too late, honey. He's very cold."

I sat back on my heels. "No, no, no. Not again. I can't believe it."

Jason reached for my hand and squeezed it. He took out his phone to call 911.

I TOLD THE PARAMEDICS THAT STANLEY HAD NO FAMILY to call, and the younger of the two phoned the coroner. Brian, still in his polo shirt and jeans, arrived right after that with his partner, Lisa. Lisa guided us outside to take our statements and then said we could go.

Beau was where we'd left him in Jason's car, no worse for wear from the mild evening temperature. Jason let him out to go to the bathroom and gave him some bottled water. I coaxed him to return to the back seat, and we set off for my cottage. Jason and I didn't speak. There wasn't anything to say.

Jason drove down my driveway and parked outside the cottage.

"Do you want me to come in?" he asked.

"This has been one of the longest days of my life. I think I want to go inside and try to sleep."

Jason turned around and looked at Beau. "I can take this guy home with me tonight, but it can't be long-term. I'm not allowed to have pets in my apartment."

"Let me sleep on it and see if I can come up with a solution."

Jason kissed me gently and I went inside. I thought I'd have a hard time getting to sleep, but I fell onto the bed without brushing my teeth or changing clothes and was under in seconds.

THE NEXT MORNING, I AWOKE WITH two thoughts: Who had killed Trudy and Stanley, and what to do about Beau? Brian's partner, Lisa, had promised to let me know if they found a will or any instructions for the dog. In the meantime, I decided Beau could come live with me.

I met Jason at his apartment a couple of hours later, prepared to take home another pet. Beau lay in a huge bed on the floor, his head between his paws.

"You're sure about this?" Jason asked.

"Yeah. In for a penny, in for a pound. Like a dog pound. Ha, ha."

"He's a good old thing," Jason said. "I don't think he'll give Sugar and Flour any trouble."

"That's not what I'm worried about. I'm worried they'll give *him* trouble. He's not exactly a spring chicken, and they're two lively three-year-olds." I laughed. "Hopefully it will all work out."

"I went out earlier and bought everything he should need. I've fed him and walked him too."

"Thanks. That's a big help."

We loaded Beau's things into the mini-van and then came back for him and his bed. I settled into the driver's seat and lowered the windows.

Jason leaned in and kissed me. "How are you doing?" he asked softly.

"I can't believe it happened again. Do you think Brian and Lisa are suspicious of me? Everywhere I go, I'm finding bodies."

"I don't think so. If they were, they'd have dragged you down to the police station. But it's pretty obvious the two murders are related."

"Jason, I need to talk to you more about this. I'm worried I played a part in Stanley's death. But I want to get Beau home, okay?"

Although he looked alarmed by my suggestion that I was somehow at fault, Jason nodded, and I drove off. Fifteen minutes later, I parked in my usual space outside the cottage. I took Beau by the leash and opened the front door.

"This, my friend, is your new house, at least for now. Think of it as a vacation home."

I removed the leash. Beau sauntered into the living room and settled onto the bare floor. The poor guy was clearly exhausted. I unloaded his things from the mini-van and brought them inside.

Beau climbed into his bed just as Sugar and Flour bounded into the room to see me. They immediately caught sight of Beau and went over. Beau sleepily lifted his nozzle and sniffed them. They sniffed him back, beginning with his head and ending with his tail. They seemed to sense he was more friend than foe, and a mere few seconds later, they'd curled up in the bed beside him. He appeared to take their presence in stride.

The sight of the three animals together touched something deep inside of me. On the one hand, the pets were so adorable together; on the other, I couldn't stand that each of them had lost, in one way or another, the humans who had loved them. I promised myself they would get all the love I was capable of giving them.

"IT'S SO CUTE," I TOLD JASON on the phone later. "The cats and Beau are already best pals."

"That's great."

"I'm gonna take Beau for a walk later. A short one. We'll have to get into a routine."

"It's sweet of you, honey. You're taking on everyone."

"Yeah. And I love that. But I'm pretty tired of it happening because someone has been killed."

"I hear you. This has to stop," Jason said, his tone turning serious.

"It's national news now. I saw it in the New York Times online. Still no leads, though, on Trudy or on Stanley, according to Isabella. She talked to Brian."

"I overheard some tourists talking about it at the restaurant. I'm afraid people are going to stop coming to Oceanville."

"That would be so bad. We need the tourists."

Jason let a couple of beats pass before saying, "Kayla, what did you mean when you said you felt you played a part in Stanley's murder?"

"Did you recognize the scarves? The one Beau was wearing and, more importantly, the one around Stanley's neck? The one that was used to strangle him? Those are the scarves I left for him yesterday morning. I provided the murder weapon!"

"Honey, the only person responsible for this is the killer. It's not your fault."

I wasn't convinced. "I guess I better get to work."

Jason said he had to go, too, and we hung up.

AFTER I FINISHED A CAKE FOR an office party and fed all the pets, I decided it was time for Beau's walk. I attached his leash and he looked up at me happily.

"Our first walk," I said. "Very exciting."

The cats circled around us.

"I'm sorry, sweethearts. This is something that Beau and I will be doing on our own. Unless you want leashes attached to you, which based on your dislike of collars, would not work at all. But this guy is much older than you, so we won't be gone long."

I grabbed a plastic bag and we set out.

Once Beau had done his business and we'd reached the coastal path, Vicky and Angie came walking toward us. Angie ran up to scratch and pet Beau. He accepted her affection gladly, his tail wagging briskly.

"Hi, Angie. Hi, Vicky. How are you guys?"

"We're good," Vicky said. "Getting back to our normal routine after Angie's party. That's Stanley Young's dog, Beau, isn't it? What are you doing with him?"

"Taking care of him for a while." I gestured at Vicky to step over to the side of the path while Angie was engaged with Beau. "Stanley was attacked," I said quietly. "He's dead."

Vicky drew in a sharp breath. "I hadn't heard. I can't believe it."

"I know."

Angie skipped over to us and asked if she could take Beau down to the beach. We agreed. Her mother told her to stay in sight, a little harsher than she might have if she hadn't just heard the news about Stanley.

"It was the same kind of thing," I said. "Strangled with a scarf. The scarf, I am horrified to add, that I left for him earlier in the day."

"This is beyond words," Vicky said. "It's beginning to feel dangerous to live here. Will we not be able to go for walks anymore?"

"I know it feels like that. But I firmly believe Trudy's and Stanley's murders are related in some way. Try not to worry. The police are going to work it all out. Or I will. Listen, Topher and Laura have alibis. Do you have any more thoughts? Especially now that you know Stanley was attacked?"

"The only thing I can think of is I saw Trudy and Stanley together at the clubhouse restaurant a day or two before she died. I forget which night. They were friends, weren't they? It's not like that would have been unusual." Vicky glanced down at the beach at Angie and Beau.

I considered. Yes, Trudy often went to the clubhouse restaurant with friends. She and I usually didn't go together because she knew I liked to visit with Isabella when I was there. It wouldn't have been unusual for her to meet up with Stanley for a meal, but it could be significant. I wondered if Isabella had been their waitress.

"Also, you might want to talk to Dana Kim," Vicky said. "She and Trudy used to be friends in the knitting club, but I noticed they weren't as friendly anymore. They stopped sitting next to each other in the last few weeks before Trudy died."

I thanked Vicky for the tips, and we went down to the beach to play with Beau and Angie.

"Look what I found," Angie said, holding up a scruffy yellow tennis ball. "Will he chase after it?"

"He's pretty old," I said. "You can try." I removed Beau's leash.

She threw the ball a short distance in front of us and Beau loped off. He brought the ball back to Angie, his eyes bright and his tail wagging, and they repeated the process. Vicky and I looked at each other, pleased. We might have a crazy killer loose, but at least we had our pets.

After a few more throws, Beau lay down in the sand and yawned, so they stopped.

"I'd better get going," I said, reattaching Beau's leash. "You guys are coming to the holiday party, right?"

"We wouldn't miss it," Vicky said.

"I'm going to be a reindeer. My costume is really soft and furry," Angie offered.

"That sounds great. I haven't decided what to be yet," I said.

"Are you going to bring Beau?" Angie asked. "He could wear reindeer ears like in *How the Grinch Stole Christmas*."

I laughed. "That would be cute, but I don't think he'll want to come to the party. He likes quiet and no crowds."

"Is he an HSP?" Angie asked.

"He may well be," I said. "You don't mind the holiday party?"

She shook her head vehemently. "I like the desserts and the decorations. And everyone dressing up."

"Then she gets tired, though," Vicky said.

"Sounds exactly like me," I said. "HSPs forever." I put out my knuckles and Angie and I fist bumped.

I added, "I'm providing some of the desserts, so be sure to look me up."

Angie bobbed her head up and down.

"See you soon." I took Beau by his leash, and after complimenting him for a successful outing, off to home we went.

Once we were home and Beau had settled down in his bed, I called Isabella. She remembered Stanley and Trudy eating at the restaurant the day Vicky had mentioned, but she hadn't been their waitress. She had no idea what they'd talked about. She went off to ask the other waitstaff. When she came back on the phone, she said they didn't even remember seeing Trudy and Stanley. I thanked her for trying.

"Hey, are you going to the tree lighting tonight?" Isabella asked.

"Oh my gosh. I forgot all about it. I already delivered my desserts yesterday before meeting Jason for dinner. Yeah, I'm going. I might be able to talk to a few people. Maybe Cliff the gardener will be there, and I can follow up on his alibi. You?"

"No. I have to work. Stop by to say hi, if you can."

"I will."

CHAPTER 9

Like Isabella, Jason had to work that evening, so he couldn't attend the tree lighting ceremony with me. I arrived solo to the clubhouse's courtyard and looked up in wonder at the fifty-foot tree. Every inch was covered in huge red and silver balls.

I checked on my pies and cakes at the dessert table. Everything looked good, so I went back to gaze at the tree.

A woman who looked to be in her seventies with a jaunty Santa hat on her head walked toward me. Besides the Santa hat, she wore a green bell on a red cord around her neck, which signaled her arrival like a cat.

"Hello, there," she greeted me. "You're the baker, aren't you?"

"Yes. Kayla Jeffries."

We shook hands.

"I'm Freida Jimenez. From the Seaside Shores Board of Directors."

Freida's introduction triggered the memory of Laura Fremont saying Trudy had an in on the board which led to her observatory being approved. Time to find out about that.

"I was hoping to talk to someone from the board," I said. "I understand Trudy Dillingham's request to construct an observatory in her backyard was approved."

Freida nodded.

"I didn't think that kind of thing was allowed because it could either disturb the look of the neighborhood or block someone's view," I said. "I'd like to use her plans and have one built in my own yard."

"It all depends on the size of the proposed building. Ms. Dillingham's astronomy tower wasn't going to show over her fence. It wouldn't have impacted anyone's view and no one would necessarily even know about it. We approved it unanimously."

So Laura and Topher's view of the water wouldn't have been blocked by Trudy's observatory, after all. Interesting. Meanwhile, I felt a rush of relief knowing that Trudy hadn't blackmailed someone on the board to get her request approved, an unpleasant idea I'd been turning over in the back of my mind.

"Just pick up the paperwork at the office and turn it in," Freida said.

I didn't intend on building an astronomy tower in my small back patio, but I thanked Freida and directed her to my apple pies on the dessert table. She smiled and hurried over. Pie had a way of eliciting that reaction.

I spotted Dana Kim, the community's CFO, across the courtyard. Remembering Vicky's tip about Dana and Trudy's falling out, I went over.

"Hi, Dana," I said. "I hope you try the apple pie or chocolate cake. I made them. Let me know what you think."

This was a pretty silly ploy since she was already carrying a plate with both a piece of pie and a slice of cake. She held up the plate and looked at me like I didn't have any crust on my pie.

"Oh good, you have some. Do you like them?"

"They're absolutely delicious, Kayla. I'm so glad I ran into you. My sister's birthday is coming up, and she always feels the occasion gets lost in the Christmas shuffle. Do you think you could design a special dessert for her?"

"Sure." I slipped a business card from my messenger bag. "Give me a call or email me. By the way, I heard that you and Trudy used to knit together in the club."

"That's true." Her sunny enthusiasm over my baking faded. "We had a fight a while back, though."

"You did? What about?"

Dana didn't look me in the eye when she said, "You know, I don't even remember. Something silly, I'm sure. I'm devastated that we didn't make up before she died." She lifted the pendant on her necklace and twirled it in her fingers.

The lack of eye contact and the way she was fiddling with her necklace made me think she was lying and that she knew exactly what the fight was about. Before I could ask any more questions, she excused herself and hurried off.

After Freida Jimenez flipped the switch to light the tree and everyone had exclaimed over how beautiful it was, I stopped by the restaurant to say hello to Isabella and then headed home. I hadn't seen Cliff, but I felt it was a promising investigative evening, nevertheless. At home, I added what I'd learned to my logic grid.

THE NEXT MORNING, BRIAN'S PARTNER, LISA, emailed me. I'd asked her to let me know if the police found anything in Stanley's house detailing his wishes for Beau. She told me that Stanley didn't have a will, nor had he left any written instructions for his dog.

That was the bad news. However, there was good news too:

I've been thinking of getting my grandmother, Stella, a pet. She's been lonely after my grandfather died. An older dog like Beau would be perfect for her. May I give him to her?

I wrote back right away to say it was a terrific solution and that I could meet them later that afternoon to hand off Beau. As fond as I was of the old dog, the cottage was feeling a little cramped with him and the two cats. Plus, finding time to walk him was getting to be a problem.

After finalizing the arrangements for getting Beau to Lisa and her grandmother, I took out the mini-van to deliver the cake I'd made for the office party, which was scheduled for lunchtime. Back at home, I shut myself in the kitchen to work on a birthday cake order.

Once I'd taken the chocolate cake out of the oven and placed it on a cooling rack, I washed a few dishes, looking out the kitchen window to the ocean as I scrubbed. We were having another mild December without much rain, a worrisome development as California was always susceptible to drought. But the sun sparkled off the water and I was glad for the moment that it wasn't raining.

From my vantage point, I could see the coastal walk. A few people passed by, including a woman I recognized as Dana Kim. I'd been hoping for another opportunity to talk to her. I pulled open the kitchen door and hurried outside, crossing the driveway and planked walkway in record time.

"Dana!" I cried, running after her on the path. "Dana!"

The woman stopped walking and turned around. And . . . it wasn't Dana.

"I'm so sorry. I thought you were somebody else. Sorry to bother you."

Since I was there, I took a short walk. I listened to the waves and the muted sounds of children down at the beach laughing when the cold surf hit their legs. Sea lions bellowed, adding to the music of the ocean landscape. I looked out at the blues and greens of the sea and tasted the salty air on my lips. In a buoyant mood, I returned to the cottage.

Flour and Sugar greeted me at the door. My American shorthairs looked particularly . . . white. They were always white, of course, but they seemed even whiter than usual. On closer inspection, I saw they were covered from head to tail in flour and sugar. My mouth dropped open. I remembered with a kick to the gut that I'd left the door to the kitchen open. I tiptoed to the kitchen, apparently thinking that if I went quietly, everything would be fine. No such luck. The floor was covered in white paw prints. My flour and sugar bins were upended, their contents spread across the counter and onto the floor.

I looked down at the cats, who had followed me. "Okay, guys. This was partly my fault. It's very fitting the way that you got into the flour and sugar because of your names. But it's a good thing I don't have an inspection coming up soon."

I calculated the work ahead of me. I'd need to order more flour and sugar from my supplier and buy some at the grocery store to get me by until it arrived. Obviously, the kitchen would require a good cleaning. I'd start after I took care of the cats.

Closing the door to the kitchen so the cats couldn't cause further damage, I went back into the living room, the two trailing after me. I took Sugar into my lap and brushed her. But the flour and sugar were matted in her fur. I tried the same thing with Flour with the same result.

They were rather agitated, and I had to face the facts: these cats needed a bath.

After obtaining some advice from the trusty internet, I proceeded to bathe them separately in the tub. I couldn't believe it when they ended up in the warm water together, happily dog paddling around the small space. I laughed and praised them.

They at last grew tired of being in the water. I took them out by turn and dried them with a fluffy towel. Once they were back to normal, they ran off and curled up on the bed, exhausted by their grand adventure. I returned to clean the kitchen, checking the clock to see that I didn't have much time before I was to hand off Beau to his new owner. After that, I'd go to the store to get temporary supplies. I'd have to finish the birthday cake the next morning, as I had a dinner date with Isabella.

I MET ISABELLA AT AN ITALIAN RESTAURANT in downtown Oceanville at six. I told her about the cats getting into the sugar and flour.

"That's funny," she said, "but it must have been stressful too." She grabbed a roll from the basket on the table. "How come you're not more upset?"

"It could have been worse. They didn't break anything. They just pushed over the plastic flour and sugar bins and the lids came off in the process. They didn't get to my cake-in-progress. I ordered new sugar and flour from my supplier on a rush order and bought some at the store to get me by. The cleanup wasn't particularly harder than it normally is."

"That's good."

I took a deep breath and said, "I gave Beau away."

"Yeah, Brian mentioned that Lisa wanted to give him to her grandmother. Was it sad?"

"It was, but Beau and Stella hit it off right away. I think they'll be good for each other. Meanwhile, Lisa confided in me that they have no new leads on Trudy's or Stanley's murders. Their working theory is the same person strangled both of them, which seems obvious to me too."

"What are you going to do next?"

"I don't know. If you think of anything, I'm open to suggestions. Don't tell Brian."

She smiled. "No way. He may be my guy, but you're my best friend."

"Thanks."

"Speaking of boyfriends, how's Jason?"

A warm feeling came over me. "He's good. Really good. I think we might be on to something serious."

"I think Brian and I are also on the way." She grabbed my arm across the table and squeezed it.

"Whatever happened with Jack?" I asked.

"Oh, that. It petered out as quickly as it began. It's Brian all the way. Hey, we could have a double wedding. And you would make the cake, of course."

"Maybe we're jumping ahead a little too much?" I said, laughing.

Still, I couldn't help sharing Isabella's enthusiasm. If only Trudy were alive. She would have been so happy for me that I'd found a new boyfriend. Then I remembered she had blackmailed that very boyfriend. Would I ever come to terms with who she was?

CHAPTER 10

As soon as I walked in the door after dinner with Isabella, my phone rang. Speak of the devil. It was Jason inviting me to go to a tree farm the next day. I had to frost and decorate the birthday cake I'd started, but had no other orders to fulfill. I accepted.

Jason showed up at eleven the next morning in a Christmas sweater with a drunk reindeer on the front, and I burst out laughing.

"Pretty awful, right?" he asked as he looked down at himself.

"No, actually. I like it." I put my arms around him and pulled him close. When it came to Jason, I didn't have any problems with personal space.

After we'd exited the embrace, he said he'd be right back and went out the front door. He came back a moment later with a package gift-wrapped nicely in holly paper, which he handed to me.

"A Christmas present? Already?"

"Sure. You deserve it."

We sat on the couch, and I undid the thick ribbon. Sugar and Flour came running. I threw the ribbon on the floor for them and they pounced on it. I opened the package and removed a soft red Christmas sweater. Tastefully done, and not at all an "ugly sweater," it featured two cats playing with a ball of yarn near a Christmas tree. The cats looked like Sugar and Flour.

"I love it," I said. "Thank you."

"Are you ready to have a little lighthearted fun today?" Jason asked. "I say we need it after everything that's happened lately."

"I think you're absolutely right. To that end, I'm going to wear my sweater."

I put on the sweater, found it to be a perfect fit, and we left.

After much discussion, we chose small trees for Jason's apartment and for my cottage. Together, Jason and I hefted them into the bed of the pick-up truck he'd borrowed from his sous chef. Then he drove us to a cute café decorated with multi-colored lights and poinsettias of different shades. We had lattes and shared a scone while looking out, satisfied, at the trees in the truck.

THE CATS WERE BESIDE THEMSELVES WITH excitement when we brought my tree indoors. They ran between our legs and almost made us trip. Jason and I found it extremely funny, and we laughed so hard that we dropped the tree.

I gave the cats a few treats to distract them. Once Jason had secured the tree in the stand I'd unearthed from my storage shed, we backed up to admire his handiwork. The cats watched from the couch, where they'd finally settled down.

"Does it look straight?" Jason asked.

"Yep. Good job."

"I hope you have non-breakable ornaments," Jason remarked. "The cats are gonna be playing with anything that's on this tree."

"Good point. Callie, the cat I had when I was younger, never cared about the Christmas tree. But these ones clearly do. This afternoon, when you're back at work, I'll stop by the ornament store. Do you think they'll take down the entire tree?"

"I guess you'll find out." He grinned. "You can call me if you need me to put it upright."

"Thank you."

LATER, AFTER JASON HAD HUNG A FEW STRANDS of outdoor lights along my gutters and returned to work, I swapped my new sweater for a blue cardigan and left in the mini-van for the shops in downtown Oceanville. I parked in a public lot and headed for the ornament store.

Apparently, this was the place to be; patrons took up every inch of space in the store. I knew Audra, the owner, because I'd done the desserts for her daughter's quinceañera. I was happy to see that business was booming.

When Audra had a break in customers at the cash register, I went over.

"Hey, Kayla. Good to see you." Audra, a brown-eyed blonde like myself, smiled at me.

"Good to see you, too, Audra. I seem to have acquired two rambunctious young cats, and I need some non-breakables."

"Oh, how fun. Okay. They're over in that section." She pointed across the store. "You know, I meant to contact you. I was so horrified to hear about Trudy."

"I know. It was unspeakable."

"I ran into her a few days before it happened. I asked if she was going to stop in this year, and she said no. It was a little odd. She always loved looking at my new selections. She seemed sad."

I'd completely missed the fact that Trudy hadn't decorated yet. Like clockwork, she began decorating for Christmas on November first. Every year, she enjoyed shopping for more ornaments. But she hadn't put up as much as a candy cane this year. What did it mean?

A few customers had lined up behind me, so I couldn't ask Audra any follow-up questions. I made my way through the crowds to the non-breakable ornaments. I was happy to find a number of charming moose and reindeer wearing sweaters and scarves.

I didn't have a chance to talk to Audra again. When I went up to the counter to pay, several people gathered behind me. Audra and I only had time for business. She wrapped up my purchases and waved good-bye.

On the drive home, I couldn't help wondering if Trudy had known her days were numbered. I wanted to talk to Isabella and get her take.

AFTER I DROPPED THE ORNAMENTS OFF at the cottage, noting that the tree was still standing, I set out on foot for the clubhouse restaurant. Clouds were gathering above and the wind had picked up. Feeling chilled, I pulled my cardigan close.

I ordered a decaf peppermint mocha from Isabella, and a few minutes later, we were seated at a window table.

"What do you think it means?" I asked her. "Why didn't Trudy want to decorate?"

"I guess she just didn't feel the Christmas spirit this year." Isabella looked out at the ocean and I followed her gaze. The clouds had formed into dramatic shapes. No one was braving the beach as waves crashed into the shore. "Did you gather she was a little lackluster?" she asked.

"No," I said. "I'd like to think I would have noticed. It's strange. I wonder if she was ill. Did she think she would die soon and this monster came along and took care of it himself? I wasn't aware of her going to any doctor's appointments. She didn't even take medication."

"I think she would have told you if she was sick. Listen, I have to go do a few things. I'm leaving early. Brian and I have a date. I think he's going to propose."

I almost sputtered coffee through my nose. "What did you say?"

"Brian's going to propose. He asked me out to Marina 44, and you know how fancy that place is. Maybe he'll have the ring placed in the crème brûlée. What? What's the matter?"

I wasn't sure where to begin. "Look, I know we were discussing the idea of a double wedding, but I thought we were talking a long time from now. Don't you think it's a little soon?"

"When you know you've found the one, it's never too soon."

I gulped. I certainly didn't feel I was ready to marry Jason. Thinking back, I remembered that Isabella started dating Brian only a few weeks before I met Jason.

"It's okay. I can tell you don't approve," Isabella said coolly.

"Just think about it, Iz. You guys don't know each other that well. And until recently, you'd been dating Jack as well."

"Yeah, I know, but that thing with Jack was over as soon as it began. Brian is a good guy, Kayla. He cares about justice. He volunteers at a women's shelter. He's really nice to me. Most importantly, he doesn't have a sexist bone in his body."

I nodded. He did seem like a great guy.

"I'll let you know as soon as I can." She'd easily moved on from her coolness. Her eyes were bright with excitement.

I tried talking to her about where to go next with my investigating, but I could tell her heart wasn't in it. She was a girl ready to become a fiancée. I hoped our relationship wouldn't change too much if she did get engaged. I'd already lost Trudy and didn't want to lose her too.

At home, I located my indoor Christmas lights in the storage shed and threaded them through the tree. I hung my new ornaments as well as a few non-breakables I already had. One of my favorites was a caroler made from yarn that my mom had given me when I was a teenager. I also unearthed some ocean-themed ornaments—an otter, a seal, and a whale.

I turned on the TV to a seasonal radio channel and listened to carols at a low volume while I decorated. I had a complicated relationship to music. Some songs I loved. I'd been known to dance around my house to an upbeat tune. A few haunting melodies grabbed me deep in my soul and brought me to tears no matter how many times I listened to them. Other songs grated at me and I immediately had to turn them off. The carols were just right and put me in a festive mood.

Once I'd finished the tree and was on the couch studying one of my cake decorating books, the cats tumbled into the room. Their eyes grew wide when they saw the tree had ornaments now. They hurried over and batted at the ones on the lower branches. Three ornaments came off, but no harm came to them.

While the cats played with the ornaments, I went into the kitchen to experiment with making truck-shaped cookies with trees in the back, inspired by the memory of my day with Jason. I was quite pleased with the result and decided to bake a big batch for the holiday party. Determined to change Vincent's mind about ordering desserts from me, I made a mental note to take some to the clubhouse restaurant to give to him.

When I had yet to hear from Isabella about her proposal, I packed up a small box of cookies and went looking for her at the clubhouse restaurant the next morning. I went in but didn't see her. Vincent accepted the cookies and a business card without a fuss—a good sign, I felt.

I left and walked along Isabella's route, looking for her in case she was on the way. No luck. Finally, I went to her rental house and rapped on the door. She answered wearing candy cane flannel pajamas, her hair caught up in a messy bun.

"I've been looking for you everywhere," I said. "Why aren't you at work? Are you sick?"

"I'm going in later. No surprise, Vincent was annoyed, but I never call in sick. I have tons of leave I've never used. He has no right to be upset." She went to the kitchen and sipped from a mug on the counter.

"Well, what happened? How was the proposal?" If Brian *had* proposed, she wasn't very happy about it. And I'd looked. There was no ring on her finger.

"He did not propose. And we had a fight. I don't want to talk about it." She took her mug over to the couch and collapsed into the cushions. I followed and perched on the couch arm.

"I'm so sorry. But don't you agree it was a little early? And what about law school?"

"That's exactly what he said. Both of those things. And then I said I disagreed. And that's what led to our fight."

"It doesn't mean he doesn't care about you."

"Really? I told him I loved him, and guess what, he didn't say it back."

"I'm sure he just wants to absolutely mean it when he says it."

"I absolutely meant it."

In our relationship, Isabella was the one to talk *me* off a ledge. Now the roles were reversed. What would Isabella say if this had happened to me and Jason?

"I think you can fix this, can't you?" I said.

"I don't know. I don't see how I can go back now. I said if he didn't want to get married, I didn't see any point in us dating."

"Oh, Iz."

Isabella put her mug on the coffee table in front of her and covered her face with her hands. "Shoot. Have I blown it? I've blown it, haven't I? Why couldn't I have been patient? I've always been too impulsive and impatient."

"In the words of a wise woman, you need to talk to him. Communication is the most important part of a relationship."

"I can't. I have to go to work."

"When you get off work, then."

"Oh, all right." She brightened. "I'm glad we have each other, aren't you? We keep each other from going crazy with these men."

We laughed, and she left for the shower. I went home to work.

ISABELLA CAME OVER LATER. I WAS in the middle of baking, so I brought a chair into the kitchen for her. She looked even worse off than she had earlier. Normally, she was an immaculate dresser; her clothes always neat and ironed, free of stray threads or holes. Now, her shirt was dirty and her linen pants showed obvious wrinkles. Her hair was all over the place.

"Well, I found out why he doesn't want to marry me," she said, gesturing wildly.

"What? You did?"

"He has a fiancée."

My mouth dropped open. "You're kidding." I put aside my mixing bowl and led her out of the kitchen. I shut the door, and we went to sit on the couch. Flour immediately jumped into Isabella's lap, and my friend half-heartedly scratched the cat's head and chin.

"No, I'm not kidding. Okay, to be fair, they'd broken up before he and I got together, so technically she's not his fiancée anymore. But now she's back and he's seen her a couple of times. I can't believe this happened."

"He admitted he's been seeing her?"

"Yes. It's one of those we-should-try-to-work-it-out, let's-see-how-it-goes kind of things."

"Oh nuts."

"Yeah. The worst thing is he never told me about her, Kayla. Ever. I mean, not even 'I used to have a fiancée.' He misled me."

I decided this wasn't the time to bring up Jack. At least Isabella hadn't been engaged to him. "Did he say why he didn't tell you?"

"He was sure it was over and it was a sore subject for him. She cheated on him the day after they became engaged. Can you believe that? That should have been the end, right? No. She's back, throwing herself on his mercy. He's too nice. He should tell her to go jump in the ocean."

"I'm sorry."

"Look, I'm okay now about not getting engaged. I don't know what I was thinking. I can't plan a wedding. I need to keep studying for the LSAT and then apply to school. But I really like him, Kayla. I want to be with him."

I thought for a moment. Flour climbed from Isabella's lap into mine and I scratched her head. "Sit tight, okay? I bet it doesn't work out with them. She's already shown her true colors. Just be understanding and patient."

"Patience. Hmm. Not my strong suit as we know."

"If I can talk to murder suspects, you can be patient with Brian."

"I'll try."

I sent Isabella off with some of the truck sugar cookies and was gratified to get a smile out of her.

Just as I was going to bed, Dana Kim called to ask if we could have lunch the next day. She said she wanted to talk to me about something. I'd almost forgotten about her skittishness at the tree lighting when I'd asked about Trudy and how I'd wanted to follow up with her. I'd never heard from her again about a dessert for her sister's birthday. I agreed and we set a time.

Dana met me in the wharf parking lot at noon the following day. I'd seen her drive up and taken note of her car—a Toyota.

As we greeted each other, she ran her hand down her hair several times and avoided eye contact.

"Lunch is my treat," I said when we were inside Sam's, hoping that would help her relax.

"Thank you. That's nice of you."

The hostess directed us to a table on the deck and handed us each a menu. The waitress came over a few minutes later. I ordered a shrimp sandwich on sourdough bread with steak fries, while Dana asked for salmon with veggies. We both requested a salad to start. Dana began to loosen up a little when our salads arrived.

We chatted about the weather and the upcoming holidays. When there was a break in the conversation, I said, "Dana, I know this is a difficult subject, but I have something to ask you. Was Trudy blackmailing you?"

A seagull swooped down to a nearby table that hadn't been cleared yet and stole a french fry. We both shrieked.

"The gulls are fearless," I commented after my heart stopped hammering.

"Sure are," Dana said, clearly startled.

After taking a bite of salad, she said in a low voice, "Yes, she was blackmailing me. I'd confided in her that I served time in jail. She sent me a note saying I had to give her money or she'd release the information." She wiped a tear from her eye. "It wouldn't look very good if it came out that the CFO of the community is a felon."

I asked as delicately as possible, "Why were you in jail?"

"When I was twenty-one, I stole money from the shop where I was working and got caught. My parents weren't doing well. They both were ill. I needed the money."

"I'm so sorry. About that and about Trudy."

"Thanks." She grimaced. "It was such a betrayal. I thought we were good friends. I'm not sorry she's dead."

I nodded. Although I couldn't agree completely with what she'd said, I understood why she felt betrayed. I'd been feeling the same way.

"Did you pay her?" I asked.

Dana acknowledged she had with a brief tilt of her head and then used her cloth napkin to wipe away her tears.

"When did this happen?"

"A couple of weeks before her death."

That lined up with what Jason had said.

"Before you suspect me, I have an alibi," Dana said. "I was in a meeting. You can double check it, if you want."

I believed her. "I don't think that's necessary."

We shared a nice, if quiet, lunch. Other than Trudy and living in the same community, it was hard to find common ground with her. She talked a little about her job, her face lighting up, and though I was happy she liked being a CFO, it made me glad I was a baker. An important role in a company with a lot of pressure wouldn't have been a good job for me.

I paid for lunch and we set out for the parking lot.

"See you at the holiday party?" I asked.

"Yes. Thank you for lunch."

I wished her well. But a wave of frustration hit me when I'd settled into the mini-van. Although I now knew Trudy had blackmailed at least two people, I didn't have a definitive explanation for why and had no idea whether or not it related to her murder. Would I ever discover who had killed her?

CHAPTER 11

JASON WAS SEEING PAULA FOR DINNER the next night. Before he left to pick her up, he called me to say good-night. We had a nice conversation and arranged our next date. I hung up, happy he was in my life.

I went through my cupboards and found them bare—aside from a surfeit of baking ingredients. I didn't think I should have cake for dinner, so I went down to the clubhouse restaurant, craving a turkey sandwich. Isabella rushed over when she saw me.

"Guess what?" she asked.

I put my finger to my chin. "Let me see. Brian broke up with the ex-fiancée?"

"Yes. You were right. I held tight. And she blew it all on her own."

"That's great, Iz."

"I'm so happy. Now we're back together for the holidays. Fa, la, la, la, la . . ."

"Excellent. Can I have a turkey sandwich and fries?"

"Of course," she said. "A side salad too?"

"Please."

Fifteen minutes later, Isabella brought my sandwich and sat with me. Vincent made a show of banging his head against the wall, but once again she mouthed "break" to him and he gave up.

"Do you know if he's decided to order from me?" I asked Isabella as soon as Vincent left for the kitchen.

Isabella shook her head. "I'm afraid it's a no-go. I don't know why, other than he's a stubborn old mule."

Vincent was hardly old, in his forties at most, but I didn't correct her. The idea that I couldn't convert him to a satisfied customer dampened my mood a little, but Isabella was so elated over Brian that I soon perked up.

TWO WEEKS BEFORE CHRISTMAS, AND I was seeing more and more of Jason—which was great—but I was no closer to determining who was behind Trudy's and Stanley's murders. I brought out my logic grid and spent some time going over it. Forty minutes later, I had no answers and needed to get a move on.

Jason was due for dinner in a few hours, and then we were going to see the town's production of *A Christmas Carol*. After toying with a number of ideas, I finally decided to make a vegetable pie. I wasn't a great cook, but baking dozens of apple pies had honed my crust skills. I already had the ingredients to make a crust, but the cupboards were still bare of dinner materials, as were the fridge and freezer.

I drove to the nearest store for veggies and cheese as well as a few frozen dinners to get me by until my next grocery shopping.

Back at home, I baked my crust and filled it with veggies and cheese. With the pie in the oven, I left the kitchen and tidied the house. It didn't take long. I felt uneasy with clutter, so I was "a place for everything, everything in its place" type of girl.

After I'd dusted a little, I put on clean jeans with a white snowflake sweater. I pulled my hair back into a low ponytail and applied some makeup.

Jason arrived promptly at six, looking handsome in a green sweater and dark jeans. He handed me a bouquet of roses with a few boughs and pinecones mixed in.

"Thank you. They're beautiful." The bouquet smelled heavenly. I turned to leave for the kitchen to find a vase, but he pulled me back to give me a long kiss.

Jason was complimentary of both the veggie pie and the truck cookies I served for dessert. He was all smiles as we drove to the theater, making me even happier than I already was.

As we waited for the play to begin, Jason's smile faded when a slender bearded man wearing a red sweater over a red tie passed by our row. The man noticed Jason at the same time, and they gave each other an icy look. Whoever it was seemed to be pretty popular, and tons of people stood to shake his hand or slap him on the back as he made his way to his seat in one of the front rows.

I raised my eyebrows at Jason, who looked like he'd just received a bunch of coal in his stocking.

"Who is that?" I whispered. "A local celebrity?"

"That, honey, is Leon Haskell."

"Oh right. I think I've seen a picture of him in the paper. Your sworn enemy in the flesh."

"Yes."

"You said you two had a history but you never explained."

The house lights dimmed, and Jason put his hand on mine. "I don't want to talk about it now. I just want to concentrate on the show. Can I tell you another time?"

"Of course."

We settled in to enjoy the show, but every so often my mind wandered. What in the world was going on between Jason and Leon Haskell? What kind of a history did they have if Jason almost hit him?

The play was excellent with nifty special effects, including fake snow that fell into the audience and a trap door in the stage from which the spirits emerged. Every time I looked over at Jason, I was glad to see him smiling again.

As we drove back to my cottage afterward, we agreed that the actor who played Scrooge was top-rate.

"The program said he's going to be in an Oscar Wilde play in the summer. Want to go?" Jason asked.

I monitored myself to see if the idea of our relationship lasting that long freaked me out. I still suffered unpleasant flashbacks of my ex, Adam. But the thought of being with Jason in the summer felt okay . . . even good.

"I'd love to," I said.

JASON CAME INSIDE AT MY INVITATION. Part of me yearned to have a bath and curl up in bed, but I also wasn't ready to say good-night. I dimmed the lights and turned on the TV in time to catch the news. Brian was on. Unfortunately, he wasn't saying they'd arrested any suspects in Trudy's or Stanley's murders. In fact, he was saying what he always said: "We're working on it. We hope to have news soon."

I muted the TV.

"I'm sorry, Kayla," Jason said. "I know how much you want someone to be arrested."

I nodded glumly.

"Hey, I think *It's a Wonderful Life* is on. Toss me the remote," he said.

While we watched George Bailey's travails, the cats arrived in the room. They looked at Jason and meowed until he moved to the easy chair. Then they hopped up and crowded onto my lap. Sugar fell off and had to be satisfied sitting next to me with her head against my leg.

Jason looked put-out, and I tried not to laugh. "Wow, I'm sorry about that."

"I should have brought them something. That was rude of me. Next time I'll bring them hamburger."

"Hey. Only if you bring me hamburger too."

"All right. The four of us shall have hamburgers. Who wants french fries and milkshakes?"

I raised my hand and Flour meowed.

"Good. Sugar will have burger only and the rest of us will have fries and shakes as well." We laughed.

At a commercial, I asked Jason, "So, what's the story with Leon Haskell?"

"Not my favorite subject, but I did promise I'd tell you. This story goes back a few years. We actually went to school together at Lakeshore High in Chicago."

"Okay. Did you fight over a girl?"

He chuckled. "No, although we did fight over something. A position on the baseball team. We were both shortstops. Only one of us could make it and it was me."

"Congratulations."

"Yeah. Leon didn't quite see it the same way. He basically made high school miserable for me. He was a popular guy. Me, not so much. Baseball was about the only thing I had going for me."

"You hadn't started cooking yet?"

"Sure, but back in those days, cooking wasn't exactly cool. Nowadays . . ."

"With all the cooking shows on TV . . ."

"It's what the cool kids do. Not at the time. So I kept my interest in cooking and baking quiet. Even so, Leon and his friends pegged me as a wimp. They harassed me and did the usual bullying stuff like wedgies and stealing my clothes after swimming."

"Oh, I'm so sorry. Then what happened?"

"After we graduated, Leon went back east for college. I headed west to Arizona State. By unfortunate coincidence, we both ended up here."

"Don't tell me he was still awful to you."

"Yes, in a more grown-up way. By the time he made it out here, I'd opened the restaurant. I received a number of bad reviews soon after he settled in, and I wondered if he was behind it. He was ... drifting. Didn't know what to do. His father was loaded, and Papa Haskell gave Leon the money to start his own restaurant. As luck would have it, Leon had an idea that took off—"

"The indoor waterways?"

Jason nodded. "And he was a pro at bossing people around. Mind you, he does no cooking of his own. He's strictly management."

"You're obviously better. You're a manager and a cook." I grinned at him.

"Thanks for the vote of confidence. His restaurant, however, is doing great."

I thought for a moment. "He's involved in the Teddy Bear Last Wishes charity, right?"

"Right."

"So he must have some good in him?"

"Don't take that at face value. He landed in some trouble with drugs that was covered up by his rich father. His father saved him from jail by getting him into community service."

"That was years ago, though?"

"Yeah, when he first came out here and was in his drifting phase. He kept up the charity work past the time he needed to, but I swear he only does it to make himself look good."

"You don't think he cares about the kids?"

"Honestly, I don't think he cares about anyone but himself. The bottom line is every time we run into each other, there's that cold war going on. That's what you witnessed."

"Why were you at his house that day Trudy saw you?" It was a question I'd been meaning to ask him.

"He baited me. He called in to the restaurant and ordered a bunch of chowder from the hostess. He knew I always delivered the catering orders. I didn't know his address and didn't realize what was going on until too late. We ended up in the front yard, yelling. Trudy must have overheard and seized the opportunity."

"Ugh to all of that."

"By the way, while I kept myself from punching him, he *did* hit me. I managed to turn in time, but he got me a little on the chin."

"What a jerk."

"Have you ever been to his restaurant?" Jason looked over to the TV. The movie was about to start again.

"About a year ago. I wasn't impressed. Sure, the waterways are cool, but it was overpriced and the food wasn't that great. And I can assure you I won't be going back now. I'm squarely a Fishes Do Come True girl."

He smiled. "Glad to hear that."

We became involved in the movie after that. By the end of the film, predictably, I was crying my eyes out. A tear or two dampened Jason's cheeks as well.

I walked Jason to the door and we embarked on a very nice kissing session.

"Your breath always smells so good," I murmured in between kisses.

"It's the peppermint gum."

I broke away from him.

"What's the matter, honey?"

"It's not you Sugar and Flour don't like. You've been chewing that gum for as long as we've known each other, right?"

"Not this same piece," he said with a grin, "but the same flavor, yeah. I've been chewing it for years."

"They don't like peppermint."

We turned to look at the cats, who were now curled up together on the couch. I gave Jason one last kiss and he left.

THAT NIGHT, I DREAMED THAT LEON HASKELL and Jason were boxers fighting each other in a big match. I sat in the audience, watching. Leon decked Jason and I screamed. Jason fell into a coma and died a few days later.

When I woke up, still halfway lost in the dream, something tugged at the back of my mind. It took me a while to drag it from my addled brain. Jason said Leon had punched him the day they got into it in the yard. What if Trudy had gotten a picture of that, as well as of Jason? What if she'd blackmailed Leon too? Leon's restaurant was super successful. Trudy conceivably could have extorted a lot of money from him.

According to Jason, Leon was not a good guy. If Trudy *had* blackmailed him, might he have killed her in retaliation? I decided to go to lunch at Scales and Fins to see Leon. I'd be breaking my promise to Jason, as well as subjecting myself to the discomfort of eating alone at a restaurant, but desperate times and all that.

After I completed a baking order for an office Christmas party and sent out a few invoices, I drove to Leon's restaurant downtown. Because it was on the early side for lunch, I was able to get a table.

Once I was seated, I looked around. The labyrinth of glass-enclosed waterways in the dining room with the multi-varieties of fish swimming through was certainly lovely. Each waterway featured different-colored lighting—red, blue, yellow, and green. I understood why the restaurant was the success it was.

I perused the menu and ordered the least expensive item, a green salad with shrimp for fifteen dollars. Leon brought it out to me himself after a lengthy wait, and I did a double take. It was tiny.

"This is the lunch salad?" I asked.

"Yes. Beautiful, isn't it?"

"Um, sure."

I was glad Leon had brought me my lunch. I'd planned on asking to speak to the owner to express my appreciation, but that would have been difficult for me to pull off given how underwhelmed I was by my meal. Time to find out if Trudy had blackmailed him.

"I'm in town to visit my aunt," I said, hoping he wouldn't recognize me from the night before, nor realize I was lying. "I heard there have been a couple of murders here."

Without my inviting him, Leon pulled out a chair and sat across from me.

"Yeah, it's true," he said. "But don't worry your pretty little head. The police have things under control."

I knew things *weren't* under control, and the police weren't making headway in solving either crime. I nodded anyway, hoping to establish rapport with him.

"Did you know the people who were killed?" I asked as I took a bite of salad.

He didn't answer and seemed to be waiting for my reaction to the meal.

To keep him talking, I said, "Good dressing."

"Everyone says so. We have the best food in all of Ocean County, hands down."

"So . . . did you know the victims?"

"Nope. Never met them. I don't make it out to Seaside Shores, where the murders happened. Too busy, either here at the restaurant or doing charity work."

"Charity work? That's nice."

"It's so important to give back, don't you think?"

"Absolutely," I said through gritted teeth, remembering what Jason thought about Leon and his charity work.

"Say, are you married?" Leon asked. "How would you like to go to dinner with me?"

I considered the invitation for a few seconds. If we went to dinner, maybe I'd get some information out of him. Would he tell me the truth about anything? He'd just said he didn't get out to Seaside Shores and he actually *lived* there. Plus, he'd probably deflect any questions by bragging about himself. There was no point in accepting.

"Thanks. I appreciate the invitation," I said. "I'm not married yet, but I'm seeing someone."

"Seeing someone isn't married. What do you say?"

"Thanks, but no. I'm happy with the man I'm seeing."

"Too bad. You would have enjoyed yourself."

I made a show of looking at my watch. "Oh nuts. Is that the time? I have to pick up my aunt. Can I get this to go, and the check?"

I gathered by the look on his face that he wasn't used to being turned down. He brought the check and a to-go box and slapped them on the table.

On the way home, I stopped by the clubhouse restaurant to tell Isabella about my lunch at Scales and Fins and my conversation with Leon.

"Do you think he's the killer?" she asked.

"Hard to say. He doesn't have any problems with lying and he's certainly a narcissist. He might feel that the rules don't apply to him. But I don't even know for sure that Trudy blackmailed him." I sighed. "I'm glad I chose baking for my profession and not investigating crimes."

"When this is all over, you can go back to concentrating on that."

"That'll be good. I better go. I've gotta bake and then Jason's coming over. See you later."

At home before I started working, I pulled up the internet and searched for Leon Haskell's name. It had occurred to me that as a well-known personality in Ocean County, he was in the news a lot. As it so happened, he'd been at a Teddy Bear Last Wishes event from 1-5 on the date of Trudy's murder, so that was that. He had an alibi, and I was back to square one.

CHAPTER 12

WHEN JASON CAME OVER THAT EVENING, before even saying hello, he got up close to me and opened his mouth so wide I could see his back fillings.

"Um. Are you trying to say you want something to eat?" I asked.

"No. I'm showing you that I'm not chewing gum. I stopped chewing it right away when you told me the cats don't like peppermint. Come on. Let's sit on the couch and see what happens."

We did as Jason suggested and waited for the cats. They arrived a moment later. Sugar leapt onto my lap while Flour jumped onto Jason's. Jason and I looked at each other in amazement.

"That was it," Jason said. "How smart of you to realize that."

"I'm so glad. I was worried about the future if . . ."

I trailed off when I realized Jason wasn't listening. He was busy scratching Flour's ears and chin. Her purring was off the charts.

"Jason?"

He didn't answer.

"Okay, I'm getting a little jealous here."

"I could get used to this," he said. "You don't climb into my lap and purr whenever you see me."

"You've never asked me to. It's not something I would categorically say no to."

We laughed. Jason threw his arm around me and I put my head on his shoulder. He stroked my hair, sending tingles down my spine. When the cats left for the bedroom, we made cocoa and went out onto my front porch. We sat in the Adirondack chairs and looked out at the ocean, which today was a dark navy blue.

I took a long sip of cocoa. "I love the sound of the waves."

"It's very peaceful. We're lucky to live in this area."

"Especially at Christmas. All the decorations and special events are so magical. Trudy loved this time of year."

"What kinds of things did she enjoy doing?"

I held up my mug. "Drinking cocoa and looking out at the ocean. Knitting mittens and scarves. Decorating." I paused. "But was that her true nature? I don't know anymore."

"You seem sad about that."

"I am."

"Kayla, people can be many things at once, you know. You are, I am. I have hidden depths you can't even imagine."

"I look forward to learning about those."

"So you will. In due time."

"I hope the murderer is caught soon. Then I can relax and enjoy the season, and concentrate on learning about your hidden depths."

He leaned over and kissed me. "It'll happen."

I nodded, wondering where I could go next with my investigations. The police were getting nowhere.

THE HOLIDAY PARTY WAS FAST APPROACHING. When I told Isabella over the phone the next morning that I didn't have a costume yet, she called an emergency meeting. I obediently left for the restaurant to talk to her.

"What were you thinking?" she demanded before I'd even sat down. "I've been planning my Mrs. Claus outfit for weeks."

"I've been slightly busy, Iz, with the holidays, baking, and finding out what happened to Trudy. I think I want to go as an elf."

"That's cute. What about Jason?"

I sat at a table by the window. Isabella followed and took the seat across from me.

"He has a Santa costume from an event the restaurant hosted a few years ago," I said.

"You'll both look fabulous. Brian was going to be Santa, too, but he might have to work. So, honestly, I'm having second thoughts about going. What good is a missus without a mister?"

"Come on. It'll be fun. You can be Ms. Claus. Who's to say she has to have a husband? Maybe she's not Santa's wife. How about his sister or daughter? She can be the feminist of the family."

I thought this would be perfect, as Isabella was very into women's rights, especially at the restaurant. When she'd found out the male employees made more than their female counterparts, she threatened Vincent she'd go to the ACLU if he didn't immediately raise the women's salaries. He'd done it, but it was probably why he and Isabella had been at odds ever since.

"Good idea," she gushed, and I knew I'd said the right thing. "Okay. I'm picking you up around two thirty after lunch service is over. We're getting your costume. Be ready."

"I will. I have to deliver an order for an office Christmas party, but I'll be back."

ISABELLA WAS RIGHT ON TIME. We drove in her VW Beetle to the costume shop in downtown Oceanville.

Isabella was immediately drawn to the sexy Mrs. Claus outfits even though she already had her costume. She grabbed a bunch from the rack and headed for the dressing rooms.

A few minutes later, she returned wearing a short red-striped dress that showed off a lot of leg and a lot of cleavage. I had the urge to cover her with my jacket.

"What?" she said. "Do I look bad?"

"No, actually, you look terrific."

"I'm gonna get it."

"Wait. Iz, yes, you look wonderful. Is this really the look you want for a family holiday party, though?"

Her face fell. "I guess not. It's on sale, though."

"Why don't you wear what you already have for the holiday party and get this lovely outfit for a more private party with Brian?"

"Kayla, you're a genius." She grabbed me and kissed my cheek before I knew what was happening.

I found an elf costume I deemed appropriate. Isabella made a point of yawning widely when she saw it, a reaction I ignored.

We paid for our purchases and went for a stroll to the other shops. We stopped in at a small café to have a cup of cocoa and Isabella encouraged me to give the owner my card. I did, and told him I'd follow up after the holidays were over. He seemed receptive, so I possibly nabbed a new client in addition to a costume.

Jason called later, and I told him I'd bought my costume.

"That's great, Kayla. I have my Santa costume ready to go."

"I can't wait. It's going to be fun."

"It will. Now, I have another subject to discuss."

I nabbed a sugar cookie from the kitchen, shut the door again, and sat on the couch. "Okay. Shoot."

"One thing you might not know about me is I'm part of a caroling group."

"You're right. I didn't know that."

"We go out caroling one night every Christmas season. In fact, we go through Seaside Shores and we're going tonight. Would you like to join us?"

I laughed. "You clearly have never heard me sing. I can't sing, and I don't sing unless I'm in the comfort of my own home or a family member's. Why would they let me join anyway?"

"We're allowed to bring a plus-one. I want you to be my plus-one. You don't have to be a professional."

"I'm not even sure I can carry a tune, but I accept."

THAT NIGHT, JASON AND I MET UP with the other carolers at Fishes Do Come True, where I was handed a packet of lyrics. Good. I didn't have to know the words by heart. Jason took my hand and promised to stay close.

We were a lively bunch as we walked to Seaside Shores. Everyone was laughing and joking and swapping stories of previous Christmases. The ocean seemed to be feeling just as merry, glowing bright blue under the moonlight. Smarty Pants Jason told me this was an effect of "bioluminescence" produced by "phytoplankton" in the water.

Once we arrived in Seaside Shores, one of our first stops was an opulent home right at the water. Twin red BMWs were parked along the circular driveway.

"Nice," Jason said when he saw the cars. "If you'd like to get me one for Christmas, I wouldn't say no." He was still holding my hand, and he gave it a squeeze.

The owners of the home, a couple probably in their late fifties, came outside to listen. I recognized Mayor Chapman and remembered the pictures of him with Trudy from her scrapbook. I wondered how he was feeling about his elderly friend's death.

After we finished singing, the mayor and his wife clapped, and we moved on.

On Otter Street, we turned right onto the block of Sandpiper Lane where Isabella lived. She came out of her house with cookies, and I did a double take as I'd never known her to bake. As it happened, she was handing out cookies I'd given her earlier at the close of our shopping trip.

"You're regifting," I accused her.

"I know. But these are the best there are," she countered.

I couldn't be mad at her after that comment.

We circled around to Wave Street. In total, we sang to over a dozen houses, received lots of kudos and cookies, and had a lovely time.

Back at Fishes Do Come True, Jason served cups of cocoa and slices from one of my chocolate cakes. We sat at a table with his friends, Darryl and Mindy. Jason flung an arm around my shoulders and I smiled at him.

"You're the baker, right?" Mindy asked me.

"She made that very cake in front of you," Jason said.

"It's delicious," Mindy said, and Darryl nodded his agreement.

"Do you have a card?" Darryl asked, and I found one in my messenger bag and handed it over. This "getting out there" was sure netting me a lot of potential clients. I told them I'd follow up in January.

As might be expected, our conversation soon turned to Trudy's and Stanley's murders.

"I'm afraid to go out by myself," Mindy said. "I used to walk on my own on the beach, but I don't think it's safe anymore."

Jason and I exchanged looks.

"I think it's safe," I said. "Stanley's murder could be a result of him knowing too much about what happened to Trudy. And the same person killed them both."

"How do you know?" Mindy asked. "I haven't read that in the paper."

"Well, I don't know for sure. I'm trying to figure it all out."

"You're assisting the police?" Darryl asked, and Jason and I looked at each other again.

"Not exactly," I said.

"Remind me what you're doing for the holidays," Jason said, saving me. All talk of the murders stopped and soon everyone was trading holiday plans.

THE NEXT MORNING, I REMEMBERED I hadn't tried calling Nancy

Dougherty lately. She'd given me the pictures from Trudy's last day at the senior center and might have some helpful information for me.

I made the call, and this time, Nancy answered.

After I'd thanked her again for the pictures, I asked, "How well did you know Trudy?"

"We took a couple of classes together at the center. Spanish and needlepoint. We talked a lot."

I didn't know that Trudy had taken classes. Another revelation about her. "Can you think of any reason why someone would hurt her?"

"Well . . . I hate to tell stories out of school. It's not something I've felt comfortable going to the police about."

My heart rate picked up. Was I finally getting a break?

"Nancy, there's already been another murder that's no doubt related to hers. If there's a better time to tell a tale out of school, I don't know what it is."

"Yes, I suppose you're right. I wouldn't want anyone else to get hurt. But it's rather delicate."

Super. Another secret. "Go on."

"I'd prefer to talk in person. Can you meet me at the clubhouse restaurant?"

"Sure. I can leave now if that works for you."

We agreed to meet in fifteen minutes.

I went down to the restaurant, said hi to Isabella, and hovered by the door. Nancy arrived and we took a table.

When Nancy and I had lattes in front of us, I said, "What did you want to tell me?"

She toyed with her spoon. "Trudy had a long-term affair."

"An affair?" My heart lurched. A *long-term* affair? I'd had no idea.

"The love of her life was a prominent figure in town. Maybe his wife just found out. Or Trudy was going to reveal the information, and he needed to stop her."

"He's alive?"

"Yes. That's the thing. He was a younger man. Much younger."

"How much younger?"

"Thirty years or so."

I gasped. "You mean to say he's only in his fifties?"

"Late fifties. Yes."

"Who . . . who is it?"

Nancy looked around. No one was near us. "Mayor Lars Chapman."

I stared at her, not comprehending what she'd just told me. Then I remembered all the photos in Trudy's scrapbook. "Wow."

Nancy nodded. "Didn't you ever wonder why Trudy moved here?"

I heaved a sigh. "I guess I never thought about it. Because it's such a beautiful community?"

"Sure, sure. But it was more because Lars had recently moved in."

"Wow," I repeated.

"He and his wife were childhood sweethearts. They met when they were six. But Trudy, well, she was quite a looker, well into her fifties and sixties. I think she was too irresistible for him. The affair went on for years." Nancy stopped speaking and put her hand on mine. "Please don't ever let on I told you any of this. Trudy swore me to secrecy."

I promised. I needed time to process this information, so I paid for our coffees, got a to-go cup from Isabella along with a questioning look I didn't address, and left.

Lost in thought, I walked home. What next about Trudy? How had I missed so much of who she was? Was she a pyromaniac too? A double agent? In the Witness Protection Program? Actually, that might explain the vast gap between the Trudy I knew and the Trudy of the past. But that was too far-fetched. No, it couldn't be the Witness Protection Program.

By the time I got home, I had a plan. I went into the kitchen, secured the door, and set about making a lemon cake for the mayor. I'd give it to him as congratulations for his reelection win the previous month, allowing me the potential opportunity to learn more about him and Trudy.

Two hours later, I was on my way to the Chapmans' house, lemon cake in hand.

THE CHAPMANS' HOUSE WAS EVEN MORE IMPRESSIVE in the daytime. It was as close to being on the water as a home could get. Only one of the red BMWs sat in the circular driveway today.

I approached the giant front door and rang the doorbell. It echoed throughout the house, making me cover my ears. I didn't know how the Chapmans could stand the noise. I'd had my own doorbell disabled because every time someone pressed it, I jumped about a mile in the air.

A well-dressed woman with a bob haircut answered the door. I recognized her from caroling night.

"Mrs. Chapman?"

"Yes, that's right. How may I help you?"

"I'm Kayla Jeffries. I run a home bakery here in Seaside Shores."

She looked me up and down and I felt a rush of embarrassment for my sweatpants and ratty sweater. I should have put on the dress and shoes I'd worn on my second date with Jason. When I'd tried to return them to Isabella, she'd told me to keep them.

"We always patronize Icings Bakery in town," she said coolly.

"They're good. I am too. I brought a lemon cake to celebrate your husband's win. I'm a few weeks late, I know, but I thought I could ask him a couple of questions at the same time."

"Questions?"

"About Trudy Dillingham's and Stanley Young's murders. I wondered what the mayor is doing to ensure the safety of the community. I have a personal interest because I found them both."

Her expression closed some more.

When she didn't answer, I made a show of looking past her and asked, "Is he home?"

"No."

"Perhaps I could talk to you? Why don't we have a slice of the cake? And tea?"

I couldn't believe my forwardness, but she nodded. I should remember that this plan of action was sometimes successful.

"Come and sit in the living room, and I'll be out soon," she said.

I sat on the pristine white couch and looked out the floor-to-ceiling windows at the ocean. The windows were spotless to emphasize the effect of being on top of the water. I had a very good view of the ocean from my cottage, but this was on another level. It was magnificent.

"Nice, isn't it?" My hostess had returned.

"Nice doesn't really cover it."

"I agree."

We nodded at each other, reaching some kind of common ground.

"I don't think it's necessary to beat around the bush," Mrs. Chapman said. "Life is too short."

"I'm sorry?" I hesitated to ask what she meant.

"Have some tea." She placed the tray she'd been holding onto the coffee table and sat in a chair next to me.

She poured some tea and passed it to me. She gestured to the cream and sugar, and I liberally added them to my cup. Then she sliced the cake, placed a piece on a china plate, and handed it over. She did the same for herself, took a bite, and closed her eyes, making a few appreciative noises.

"Delicious. Leave me your card. I think we'll be leaving Icings."

"Thank you, Mrs. Chapman." I reached into my messenger bag and handed her a card.

"Call me Beverly."

"You were saying about beating around the bush?"

"I don't think you're here just to bring us a cake. Or even to ask if my husband is going to increase safety measures. Am I right?"

I nodded.

"Trudy was a friend of yours?" She locked her eyes on mine.

"Yes. We were close friends. I'm trying to work out who could have done this to her."

"Ah. So you think it might have something to do with the affair?"

I gulped. She wasn't kidding when she talked about not beating around the bush. "Right."

"I knew all about it. Not right away. It started shortly after Lars and I married in our early twenties. I found out eventually."

"You knew?"

"She was stunning. She had that type of glamourous look reminiscent of Hollywood's golden age. The wavy hair. The voluptuous figure. Despite the age difference, they made a lovely couple."

I couldn't believe how matter-of-fact she was. "You didn't mind?"

She placed her plate onto the coffee table and let a few seconds pass by. "I didn't say I didn't mind."

So she did mind. How much? Enough to kill Trudy? But why now if she'd known about the affair when it was going on? Surely Lars and Trudy weren't still seeing each other at the time of Trudy's death?

"I did mind very much. But I loved him and still do. Have you ever been in love?"

Had I? I'd thought at the time that I loved Adam. Now I realized I hadn't. I could see myself falling in love with Jason, who struck me as 180 degrees from my ex. I wasn't sure about declaring our love for each other this early, though.

"Not yet," I told Beverly.

"So you don't know. When you fall in love, get back to me. Tell me how you'd do anything for him. Look the other way time and time again. Even if he makes you promises he can't keep."

I blew out a breath as I considered that thought. It sounded depressing. "That must have been awfully difficult for you. Knowing about the affair."

"They say human beings can get used to anything. We're remarkably adaptive." She spoke pragmatically but I didn't miss the slight bitterness behind the words. "By the way, in case you're wondering, Lars and I were at a reelection party the afternoon that Trudy was killed."

"Okay." Although I hadn't read the article, I remembered seeing the headline in the Seaside Shores newsletter about a reelection celebration for the mayor at the T.A.C. I didn't know what T.A.C. stood for, but I'd had a smile over it because TAC spelled CAT backward.

We each took a bite of cake. She was left-handed, and as she brought the fork to her mouth, I took note of her engagement ring on top of a plain platinum wedding band. I recognized the singular stone in the engagement ring as an amethyst. My mother had an amethyst necklace I'd always loved.

"I could eat this whole thing," Beverly said. "Sometimes it feels so good to just let go." Her features softened, and she relaxed into her chair. She was much more human.

"There's a lot of pressure on women to look a certain way," I said.

"Yes. It's all so dreary. We should live our lives. Take our pleasures where we can. For years, I aspired to look like Trudy. I thought I could keep my husband's love that way. It was a lost cause. Maybe now everything will be different."

As if sensing she'd said too much that could be misinterpreted, she stood. "I have to get to my garden club meeting. I need to feed the cat, and then I'll walk you out."

I followed her as she headed down a hallway to the side of the house. A sliding glass door led to a patio filled with pots of gorgeous flowers. She unlocked and opened the sliding door.

"Jake!" she called. A sweet-looking tuxedo cat rushed inside the cat flap cut into the door.

"Silly," she said. "You didn't have to go through there. The whole door was open."

Beverly bent to stroke the cat, and then she led Jake and me to the kitchen. I turned green with envy when I saw the state-of-the-art oven and stoves, granite countertops, and tons of cupboards. I could only imagine the joy of baking in such a kitchen.

Beverly fed Jake some expensive-looking food, grabbed a coat and gloves from the kitchen table, and led me back to the front of the house. As we neared the front door, she turned to an alarm keypad and, cupping her hand over it so I couldn't see, punched in a few numbers. A horrendous noise sounded which was about a hundred times worse than the doorbell. We both put our hands to our ears.

"Turn it off!" I cried. "Please. I'm very sensitive to noise."

"Damn it. I forgot we changed the number." Quickly, Beverly tapped in another set of four numbers and the noise blissfully went away and was replaced by manageable beeps. We stepped outside, and she turned to lock up. We said good-bye, she climbed into the red BMW, and I set out for home.

I'D SPOKEN WITH HIS WIFE, but I wanted to have a little chat with Mayor Chapman. The next morning, I drove to City Hall, wondering if I should have tried to make an appointment first. I was directed in to see him without any trouble.

About six feet tall, with perfect posture, a well-tailored pinstripe suit, and immaculate grey hair, the mayor was a commanding presence. He stood in front of an impressive desk with a cell phone to his ear. When he saw me, he put up a finger for me to wait. I took the time to look around the office. Pictures of him with other prominent figures in town lined the walls. His diplomas from an Ivy League school were front and center behind his desk.

He disconnected the call and turned to me as I was looking over the diplomas. "Yes?"

I joined him at the front of his desk. He moved to sit in his chair.

"Hi. I'm Kayla Jeffries. I—"

"I know who you are. My wife told me you came by asking about Trudy Dillingham."

I regarded him, remembering the pictures of him with Trudy in her scrapbook. He was one of those men who became better looking with age. I wasn't sure what to make of him yet.

"You had a relationship with her," I said, taking his wife's idea of not beating around the bush.

He looked back at me for several beats. His professional demeanor lifted, and in his eyes, I saw truth.

"I was in love with her." His voice cracked a little on the last word.

"I loved her too," I answered.

We were both quiet for a moment as we thought about what Trudy had meant to us.

"I loved her but I couldn't leave my wife," the mayor said. "We have children, and I know what divorce can do to a family. Besides, Beverly has never wavered in her support of me. She didn't deserve to be left. Not that she deserved someone who couldn't be faithful either. Trudy and I broke up half a dozen times only to get back together again. Finally, Trudy cut it off for good."

I looked him in the eye. "Was Trudy going to come clean about your affair? To the press, to your constituents? That could have been bad for your career."

He waved away my statement. "Your implication is ridiculous. I would never hurt Trudy. I loved her deeply."

He was sincere. And I remembered Beverly's assertion that they'd been at a party when Trudy was killed. So much for progress in finding the killer.

I thanked Mayor Chapman and left the office, turning back briefly to see him wipe away a tear. Compassion welled up in my chest. We'd both lost something precious when Trudy died.

I DROVE HOME AND DRESSED for a walk on the beach, stewing over Mayor Chapman and his wife. It was hard letting go of them as suspects. But I believed the mayor when he said he'd loved Trudy, and his wife had known of the affair for years. So why would either kill her?

And what about their alibi of being at the reelection party?

I turned my focus to the ocean, feeling my shoulders relax and my heartbeat slow. Nature never failed to make me feel better when I was down. Despite Trudy's murder and my inability to identify her killer, I was so glad to be living where I was. It had been the right decision to move here, start a business, and find new friends.

CHAPTER 13

The next morning, I cozied up with the cats and read The Ocean County Tribune. An article caught my eye about a recent spate of break-ins in Shelltown, the city northeast of Oceanville. The burglars had broken in using cat flaps cut into wood and sliding glass doors. They'd been able to reach their arms up through the flaps and undo the locks. Besides electronics, cash, and jewelry, the thieves had stolen presents from underneath the victims' Christmas trees. I felt a rush of sympathy for the people who had been burgled at what should be the happiest time of year.

After finishing the paper and logging some payments in my software program, I took out the mini-van to deliver truck cookies to several office Christmas parties. I'd added my usual ocean-themed touch by piping seals as the truck drivers. The manager at the last delivery invited me to stay, but I declined and drove back home to do more baking.

As I tooled down the driveway to the cottage, Tristan came running out of his house waving his hands at me.

Tristan was a jolly sort, especially when he had new artwork to show off, but today he looked downright defeated by life. A wave of alarm washed over me as I stopped the mini-van and rolled down the window.

"Oh, Kayla."

"What's wrong, Tristan?"

"My art. It's ruined."

"What do you mean?" As I said it, I relaxed a little. Sometimes Tristan reacted this way when a piece wasn't going as well as he'd hoped. I knew how he felt. I often found myself in a glum mood when my decorating wasn't coming out the way I wanted it to—when a shell ended up as a fan or an otter looked more like a dog. Tristan was usually most worried about a project going south right at the point when he worked out how to fix it.

Tristan took a deep breath. "My house was broken into."

My heart hammered against my chest. "*What?*"

"They destroyed my studio. Knocked pieces over, upended my jars of tools . . . It's a disaster."

"I'm so sorry. You called the police?"

"They've all just left. Police, detectives, forensic people—the whole kit and caboodle."

"What did the burglar take?"

"Nothing. It was vandalism. Evil, evil vandalism. All the work I did. Thank god I'd already taken my pieces down to the gallery for the show."

I left the mini-van where it was. Tristan and I went inside his house so I could make him a cup of tea. When I offered to help him clean up the studio, he quietly asked me to leave. I trudged back to the mini-van and drove the two hundred feet to my cottage.

Two murders and now a break-in? I called Jason and tearfully told him what had happened. He said he would put his sous chef in charge and leave right away.

JASON AND I SAT ON THE COUCH, and I lay my head on his shoulder. The cats, perhaps sensing our stress and unnerved by it, stayed away.

"I can't believe what's been happening lately," I said. I brushed a tear from my cheek.

Jason gently pulled away from me. "Kayla, do you think it's possible they meant to break into your house instead?"

I looked back at him in shock. "What? Why? Why would you say that?"

"Bear with me and I'll explain. Have you been telling people you found Trudy? Remember, your name never made it into the media."

I hit myself in the forehead. "Yes. I'm always saying that. You're thinking Tristan's break-in was a mistake? They believed they were breaking into my house, not his?"

"I don't mean to distress you further. It's just that your house isn't visible from the street and you have the same address as Tristan. I think

Trudy's killer is looking for something. They know you found her body. Could they think you have it?"

As alarming as the idea was, I had to admire Jason's amateur detective skills.

"I don't have anything," I said.

"I know. Still, I want the police to consider this. Can I have Brian's number?"

I found Brian's card in my messenger bag. Jason took out his cell phone, and I rattled off the phone number.

After relaying his theory to Brian, Jason hung up and said, "He'll keep it in mind."

I nodded but didn't feel very safe.

We watched two Christmas movies, ate cookies, and talked. By ten, I was exhausted. Jason left, telling me to lock everything up tight and to call him immediately if I suspected I was in danger.

I MANAGED TO SLEEP, though I woke a few times when the cats rearranged themselves on the bed or jumped down to go to the litter box. When I got up in the morning at five, I was tired, but I knew I'd have to keep moving. I had baking to do and pre-Christmas deliveries to make. After the news of Tristan's break-in, I'd accomplished nothing.

Around ten, I returned home after delivering a number of orders. The front door lock yielded a little too easily. When I walked in, Flour and Sugar pulled themselves out from under the couch, their pupils big.

I saw the devastation. The couch cushions had been torn open, my fireplace grate tossed aside. Paintings were crooked. The kitchen door was open, canisters upended and cupboards left ajar, and this time I knew Sugar and Flour weren't to blame. Similar destruction met me when I toured the rest of the cottage. Jason was right. The person—the killer?—had meant to break into my house all along. I took out my cell phone and called Brian.

After I'd made my statement to Brian and Lisa, I called Jason. He was stuck at the restaurant, but he said he'd come as soon as he could. He made a suggestion that made my heart race.

With the law enforcement personnel occupied trying to gather evidence, I took note of Sugar and Flour safe under the bed and went down to the clubhouse restaurant.

Once I'd told her what had happened, Isabella settled me at a table, retrieved a turkey sandwich for me, and wrapped her sweater around my shoulders. I couldn't stop shivering. This was some serious déjà vu. We'd gone through a similar routine after I found Trudy.

Isabella sat opposite me and watched as I ate. I didn't say anything until I'd eaten every crumb.

"Jason wants to move in temporarily," I finally said. "He's worried. But I don't think I can handle that. Everything is too much right now. Too much stress, too much stimulation. I want to cry for a week and sleep for a month."

"I'm so sorry, hon. How did they get in?"

"Picked the lock like at Tristan's. Brian's going to help me get a better system. He says it was easy for them to get in. I've never worried about break-ins here in Seaside Shores, but it's all different now. Trudy had secrets, big secrets. One of them probably got her killed, and the murderer is trying to recover something of hers that he thinks I have."

"The security sounds like a good idea. Brian will get you all hooked up."

"Deadbolts, chain locks, and motion sensors. This is what has become of my life. I don't know what he's looking for. Why does he think I have it? Just because I found Trudy?"

"I don't know. But now you'll have to let the police do their thing. It's time for you to bow out."

"What? No. No way am I stopping now."

"Kayla, you can't be serious. What has gotten into you? I thought you lived for staying at home, baking, reading, and walking on the beach. Now suddenly you're investigating crimes and you're the victim of break-ins."

"I know. But, Iz, it was Trudy. Despite all the things she did, she didn't deserve what happened to her. I have to figure this out for her and for myself. Poor Stanley too."

"I don't like it. I think you should at least let Jason stay with you."

"That comes with its own set of problems. I'm not ready for a more serious relationship."

Isabella glanced over at Vincent, who raised his eyebrows at her. "Well, okay. Get all your security measures in place. Then reconsider your involvement. I don't want to lose you."

"I'll be super careful. Look, I've gotta go. As soon as the forensics team is done with the cottage, I have a huge clean-up job ahead of me. I have to order new supplies again."

"I'd help, but it's going to get busy soon. Vincent would never let me leave."

"It's okay. I'll be fine. Thanks."

THE KITCHEN ALONE TOOK SEVERAL HOURS to clean up. I ordered new supplies and made a note on my to-do list to get interim ingredients.

Next, I turned my attention to the rest of the cottage. The Christmas tree was still standing, but a few ornaments lay on the floor. That could be Sugar and Flour's doing. I hung them again and looked over at the couch. The cushions were goners. I ordered new ones online that didn't exactly match but should work well enough. I dragged the destroyed ones into my storage shed to one day take to the dump, and plumped up the decorative pillows to temporarily fill the empty space on the couch. In the bedroom, I blushed seven different shades of red when I realized the intruder had gone through my underwear drawer. My undies were strewn across the floor and I quickly gathered them up.

The security guy Brian recommended arrived about fifteen minutes later. Barry, as he introduced himself, set me up with an alarm, extra locks, and motion sensors. He taught me how to arm and disable the alarm, which was similar to the Chapmans' system. I had mixed feelings when he was done. I felt safer, but was all too aware that my innocence was gone.

As Barry was leaving, Jason arrived with Chinese food. He'd brought my favorites—moo shu chicken, egg rolls, and pot stickers—but I didn't talk much during dinner. Trudy's and Stanley's murders, the destruction of Tristan's studio, and the break-in at the cottage had me in a funk.

I didn't even accept Jason's offer to eat the last egg roll. He speared it with this fork and put it on his plate.

"Kayla, I wish you'd reconsider my moving in. Even though you have the security now, I'd feel better if I were here with you."

"Jason, I don't know . . ."

"It doesn't have to mean anything. You have a comfortable couch. We could share the cats. You and Sugar would take the bed and I'd keep Flour on the couch with me. You know how she and I have bonded." He tried for a smile.

"I don't think so."

"I want you to be safe."

"I know. And I'm not going to lie. I'm scared. There's something I was thinking I could do. Trudy thought I should sign up for a baking expo beginning Sunday in L.A. I could go for a couple of days. I have a window before I need to kick my baking into high gear again for Christmas. I might not be able to get in because it's so late, but—"

"I think it's a great idea."

"Flour and Sugar . . ."

"I'll take care of them. I'll come early in the morning and at the end of the evening."

"I've always dreamed of expanding my business. Our county is one of the few in California that allows mail orders. This event could make me new contacts."

"Do it, Kayla. I think it would be good for you to get away."

I looked into his blue eyes and he held my gaze. He really cared about me. I nodded, leaned over to his chair to kiss his cheek, and stole the egg roll.

After Jason left and I'd put all my security measures in place, I turned to my computer. I was not only able to get into the expo, I received a reduced rate because the vendor slots hadn't sold out. I booked a round trip air ticket and a room at the expo hotel without issue.

In bed later, I tried to concentrate on the Christmas-themed cozy mystery I was reading, but my mind kept returning to the break-in. I was more and more convinced that the killer was trying to find something that belonged to Trudy that he believed I had. What could it be? I didn't have anything of hers, other than the various presents she'd given me over the years. Did he think I had taken whatever it was when I found her body? I just didn't know. I finally put the book away and tried to sleep.

THE NEXT MORNING, I SHOPPED for interim baking supplies and made other preparations for the expo. In the early afternoon, I packed a small bag, removed Sugar after she jumped in, removed Flour after *she* jumped in, got the rest of my things, and went outside to wait for Isabella, who'd agreed to drive me to the Oceanville Airport.

As we drove out of Seaside Shores, Isabella took one hand from the wheel and pointed in front of us. "Look!"

"What?"

"The car ahead of us."

A Mercedes with a broken taillight was directly in front of us.

"Oh my gosh, Iz. Do you think it's the killer? Are we finally going to get a break in this case? I've been waiting my whole life to say this. Follow that car."

We were now driving along Marine Parkway, parallel to the road that led to the wharf. I wrote down the car's license plate number on the back of my boarding pass. It wasn't all that hard to keep behind the Mercedes and get the number because the car was going all of twenty-five miles an hour, even though the speed limit was forty.

Once we were able to pass, Isabella drew alongside the Mercedes. Inside were Isabella's neighbors, Donald and Mary Cohen, who were ninety if they were a day.

"Any chance one of them murdered Trudy and Stanley?" I asked.

"I seriously doubt it. I'm surprised Mary is even driving. They both have health issues and need walkers."

"So much for our car chase," I said.

"We should have known it was too good to be true."

We waved at the Cohens, who waved back. We pulled ahead of them and continued on our way.

As Isabella looked for a place at the airport curb to sneak in, I twirled my birthstone ring around my finger.

"Calm down, sweetie," Isabella said. "You're going to break off the stone."

A car left and we took its place.

"Iz, are you absolutely sure this is a good idea?"

She turned off the engine. "Look. You're on top of your orders. Jason's going to feed the cats. Maybe the murderer will be caught while you're gone. At least you'll be safe for a few days. If nothing else, I'll be able to sleep for the next two nights."

"It's going to be noisy, with a lot of people, and there will probably be fluorescent lights . . ."

"You're only there until Monday. It'll be fine. It's a good career move."

Isabella popped the trunk and we got out. I removed a box of baking paraphernalia and my messenger bag from the trunk. Isabella slung the strap of my carry-on over my shoulder and gave me a once-over.

"This is a good thing," she said. "You're promoting your business. I'm proud of you. Please don't worry. Keep calm and bake on." She smiled.

Then she hugged me tight, not caring about my personal space, and sent me off.

I WASN'T EXACTLY AFRAID OF FLYING, but I enjoyed being on the ground better than 35,000 feet in the air. I survived the short flight to Los Angeles mostly by sipping a root beer and reading my Christmas cozy mystery. I managed to get lost in the plot and was satisfied with the ending.

After I hit baggage claim and had my things, I easily found the hotel shuttle and hopped on.

In my room at the hotel, I looked out my window at the view . . . of the parking lot. It sure paled in comparison to what I had at home, but few views could compete with an ocean vista.

After resting for a bit, I headed down to the conference room to register. I said hello to a few bakers before returning to my room to read some more. Fortunately, I'd brought another mystery. I treated myself to a hamburger and fries from room service and took a bath. I slept well, though I missed the cats jumping up on the bed and cuddling with me.

The next morning, after a quick breakfast in my room, I made my way to the kitchen, where I baked a batch of sea creature cookies and decorated them. I added a touch of whimsy by piping Christmas hats onto my otters and reindeer antlers onto the sea lions. My fellow bakers were upbeat and friendly, and the smells in the kitchen were heavenly. When my cookies were done, I gathered my supplies and set up my table in the conference room. I laid out my album of designs as well as the model I'd made of Angie's birthday cake, which my fellow participants got a kick out of. It was all a little overwhelming, but fun too.

The expo opened, and I was immediately swamped. Everyone loved my ocean designs. I handed out business cards and told each person I hoped to set up mail orders soon. I received tons of compliments for my cookies.

Then, out of the blue, Isabella called. The Mercedes had been identified and the owner was in custody.

"I'LL CALL YOU RIGHT BACK," I said and hung up. I packed my things, told the baker next to me I had to go, and returned to my hotel room.

I sat on the bed and called Isabella.

When she answered, I bombarded her with questions: "Who is it? Who owns the Mercedes? How did the police find out?"

"It was the tip from Jan and Austin's son, Stewart, about the license plate. He had the letters transposed and didn't know the numbers, but they traced the car to Oscar Lancaster. Isn't that the guy you met up with at the café?"

"Yes. Trudy's boyfriend back in the day. I'm coming home."

"Only if you're sure. You haven't been there long."

"I know. But Oscar has killed two people. I want to come now."

I MADE MY GOOD-BYES TO THE ORGANIZERS, checked out of the hotel, and took the shuttle to the airport. I was able to change my flight to one leaving in half an hour. Back in Ocean County, I took a ride service from the Oceanville Airport home to Seaside Shores. On the way, I texted Jason to tell him I'd come home early and would explain soon. He texted me back, inviting me to Fishes Do Come True for dinner. I accepted.

Once I'd undone my locks and disabled the alarm, then secured everything again, I said hello to the cats. They wrapped themselves around my legs and followed me around as I settled in.

I laughed. "Okay, guys. I'm glad to see you too. I was lonely last night without you on the bed. But you like Jason now, right? Did he give you lots of food?"

I knew from the two empty plates on their food mat that he'd fed them already, but they were under the impression they should eat again. Because I loved them, and I'd missed them, I gave them each a second helping.

A knock on the door a few minutes later made my heart race. That had been a nice advantage to being in a hotel—I wasn't afraid the killer would appear at any second. It was Isabella.

"I've gotta get back to the restaurant," she said. "I just wanted to say hi and welcome you home."

"Thanks. It's good to see you, Iz. Is there anything new on Oscar?"

We moved over to the couch and sat down.

"That's the other reason I'm here," she said. "To tell you they let him go."

"What? That can't be true. Why?"

"He had a doctor's appointment at the time of Trudy's death. His daughter confirmed it. She was with him."

I shook my head, not wanting to believe another lead had fallen through. "So he's not the killer?"

"I'm afraid not, hon."

"Why had he been visiting Trudy, then?"

"He told Brian they'd gotten in touch again and become friends."

"He didn't tell *me* that," I said.

"Maybe he thought it made him look guilty. But he had to come clean to Brian."

"That makes sense," I agreed. "Darn it. This is so frustrating. I thought it was finally all over."

"I know."

"I guess it's back to the drawing board."

Isabella said, "Keep being careful, okay? As soon as I leave, lock everything up and turn on the alarm."

"I will. I promise."

After I'd locked up again and put on the alarm, I picked up my logic grid. At least I now knew the owner of the Mercedes. After I noted that on the grid, I switched to looking at my datebook. Although my schedule was clear, the holiday party was only a few days away. I wasn't due at Fishes Do Come True for a few hours, so I decided to get started. Maybe baking would help me get over the unsettling news from Isabella. My new supplies hadn't been delivered yet, but I'd shopped for interim ingredients before going to L.A.

I settled on apple pies to supplement the truck cookies I'd already planned on making. I'd wait until closer to the date to do the pies, but I could bake the cookies now. I decided to switch things up by piping otters and sharks in the driver seat instead of seals.

I closed the kitchen door and set to work, the magic of baking and creativity making me as calm as I was ever going to get.

THE CATS WERE WILD THE NEXT MORNING, batting around their noisy ball and tearing through the house. Perhaps they were celebrating my return to the household. They finally settled on either side of me on the couch and demanded my attention.

"I have to bake some more for the holiday party," I told them. "You are keeping me from work."

They were unrepentant. Whenever I tried to get up, one or the other swiped at me or grabbed my arm. I finally gave in and spent way too long petting them and scratching their ears and heads. At this rate, my business would collapse and I'd be broke. Finally, I had to take matters into my own hands and place the cats on the floor.

A TAPPING AT THE DOOR STARTLED ME as I was wrapping up the day's work. I went to the peephole and saw Tristan's smiling face.

"Just wanted to remind you about the opening tomorrow night," he said once I'd disabled the alarm and unlocked the door. Head slap. I'd forgotten about the most important event in Tristan's life. Jason and I had already made a date to go to the movies. But I'd promised Tristan.

"Of course," I said. "It's on my schedule."

"I'm so glad I'd already brought the pieces down to the gallery before the horribleness. Don't forget to bring your beau. An evening of art will make us all feel better after the break-ins."

"We wouldn't dream of missing it," I lied.

I DROVE DOWN TO FISHES DO COME TRUE to break the news to Jason about the gallery opening. He was busy bussing tables.

"Huge office Christmas party," he explained. His hair was mussed and he had bags under his eyes. This was a busy time of year for him, which was a good news/bad news kind of thing.

"It looks like it was successful," I said, pointing to the plates he was clearing. They looked like they'd been licked clean.

"Pretty much. What's up, Buttercup?"

"I know we were supposed to go to a movie tomorrow night, but I forgot I promised Tristan I'd go to his opening at SeaBlue Gallery. I'm sorry. You don't have to go. I wish I didn't."

"That sounds like fun." He took his tray of dishes into the kitchen, and I followed. "I'll be happy to go."

"No. Not fun," I said. "Not fun at all. And not happy. You haven't seen Tristan's artwork. It's weird. It's strange. It's odd. Do you understand?"

He laughed as he unloaded the tray. "Yeah. Come on, it'll still be fun. I'll go with you and take you for coffee after."

"Okay. Promise me you won't hold it against me."

"If it's that bad, the coffee's on you. And a treat too."

"Deal."

I'd given him the rundown on the expo and Oscar's release at dinner the night before. I again expressed my frustration that the killer was still out there.

"I'm sorry, honey," he said. "Please continue to be careful."

He had to call a supplier, so we kissed and I left.

CHAPTER 14

THE NEXT NIGHT, WHEN JASON AND I walked into SeaBlue Gallery, I nudged him and pointed to a corner of the room that featured Tristan's artwork. We went over.

Jason surveyed Tristan's creations and raised his eyebrows at me. "Yeah, I see what you mean. It's very out there. But that painting is nice."

He gestured to the wall at a painting of the ocean. A painting of the ocean that I decided I could not live without. If Monet had painted an Ocean County seascape, it would have looked like this: muted blues and greens of the water, reds and oranges of the sun just setting, and a couple of happy children making sandcastles on the beach.

"No way is that Tristan's," I said as we approached. My mouth dropped open when I saw his name on the plaque and his large signature in the bottom right of the painting.

"Indisputable evidence," Jason said.

"I can't believe this," I said. "I'm stunned."

While I was ogling the painting, Tristan came up to us. He wore jeans with a white shirt and a candy cane tie. Clearly in his element, his eyes were bright and his cheeks flushed.

"Tristan. Where have you been keeping this loveliness of a painting?" I demanded.

"Oh, that. I painted it years ago. I wasn't going to show it, but Jeremy thought I should."

"I have to have it. How much? No, never mind. I don't care how much. I'm buying it. I don't care if I go broke."

Tristan chuckled. "For you, doll? Nothing. You may have it. I'll put a sticker on it immediately."

"Really? Thank you, thank you, thank you." I grabbed him and hugged him, much to his surprise—and mine.

I was so giddy about the painting that I didn't mind spending time on Tristan's other artwork. But I couldn't stop peeking at my painting. Jason finally had to stop my rubbernecking and tear me away so we could leave. We said good-bye to Tristan, who promised to deliver the painting the next morning.

I was so excited and distracted that Jason got our coffees at the café to go. At home, my mood remained elevated.

Jason pulled me close. "Honey, try to calm down. You'll never get to sleep."

He knew me so well. I kissed him, promised I'd chill out, and we said good-night.

TRISTAN DELIVERED THE PAINTING the following morning, and if possible, I found it even more beautiful than I had the night before. We hung it over the fireplace. It was the perfect size.

I gazed at the painting in awe and brushed away a tear. "Thank you, Tristan. I absolutely love it."

"You're very welcome. I'm glad it makes you happy."

"I swear there's a huge market for work like this," I said. "The tourists would jump at the chance to bring home such a gorgeous reminder of their vacation. Will you consider doing more?"

He frowned. "It's so . . . obvious. So easy."

"But it's breathtaking."

"Thanks. I think I'll stick to my other stuff."

I didn't mention that none of his other work had sold, at least at the time Jason and I left. Surprising us both again, I gave him a big hug before he left, along with a few Christmas cookies.

Over the next few hours, I kept returning to the painting, even in the middle of baking. I didn't see why Tristan didn't focus on this kind of work. I was sure he'd be successful. On the other hand, I understood that he was attracted to his odd objets d'art. Once you had a creative bent, no one could talk you out of it. Fortunately for me, I was drawn to the ocean motifs I used in my work and not something out there like car parts. I giggled to myself as I imagined a cake with a carburetor on top.

I wasn't even sure I'd get the car part right. Even more fortunately, my ocean motifs were popular.

I ran into Tristan later that day on our shared driveway.

"People don't understand my art," he said mournfully after he'd confessed he hadn't sold any of his pieces.

"Don't worry, Tristan. I'm sure people will come around. In the meantime, I love my painting more than I can express."

He brightened at that. It might not have been his favorite piece, but it was still his work. He came inside with me to look at the painting again.

"It is rather lovely, isn't it?" he said, tilting his head this way and that as he looked at it.

"Don't even think of taking it back. I will fight you for it."

"Hah. I know you would. But you know I never go back on my word."

"You could paint another."

"I think I *will* consider it. I do adore the colors."

He kept looking at the painting, and I was getting the distinct feeling that despite his words, he might remove it from the wall and run away with it.

"I baked a fresh batch of the sugar cookies," I said. "Want some more?"

"Oooh, love it. Please."

I went into the kitchen and piled some cookies onto a paper plate, then wrapped them in plastic. Gently steering Tristan to the door, I explained I had pies to make.

After he left, I shut the front door, leaned against it, and nodded at the painting in satisfaction. I secured the house and went back to the kitchen to begin baking pies for the holiday party.

ISABELLA CAME TO MY DOOR LATER, and again, my heart threatened to give out until I looked through the peephole.

I disabled all my security measures and opened the door. "Hi. This is a nice surprise. To what do I owe the pleasure?"

"I'm staging an intervention," she said.

"Hmm. I don't think that one person can stage an intervention by herself."

"I don't care. I'm doing it."

"Would you like to come in? Have a cup of cocoa and some cookies?"

"No. I am not here to enjoy myself."

"Well, at least come and sit on the couch."

"I'll feel stronger if I'm standing."

I didn't feel I could sit if Isabella remained standing. The cats came over and wove between our legs.

"What is it, Iz? What in the world is wrong?"

"You have to stop, Kayla. Just stop."

"Stop what exactly? Wearing jeans instead of skirts? Making apple pies, which is what I was doing when you came over? Stop giving the cats everything they want?"

"I had a horrible dream last night that you were murdered. You have to stop investigating."

"I can't. What about Trudy?"

"Brian is handling it."

"Well, that hasn't worked very well so far. He's accomplished nothing."

"That is so unfair. He's been working overtime. We've hardly seen each other. What have *you* accomplished besides having your house and Tristan's house broken into?"

"Talk about being unfair. I've talked to people—"

"Big deal."

"It is for me."

"Don't give me that HSP stuff."

"Oh, thanks a lot. That HSP 'stuff'? You know it's real."

"Because you say so."

"This is terrific, Isabella. There are books about it, a documentary . . ."

"Anyone can invent a disorder. It's lazy. Just toughen up."

"I can't believe you're saying this. You're saying the same kinds of things Adam used to. I think you'd better leave now."

"Yeah, well, don't bother coming to my restaurant ever again."

"You can't claim the restaurant as your own. It doesn't belong to you."

"Fine. But don't expect to be in my section."

"Fine."

"Fine."

"Good-bye, then."

"Bye!"

She threw open the door and flounced out. Luckily, I hadn't armed the alarm after she came in or it would have blared and destroyed the early evening quiet. I couldn't take that as well as a terrible fight with my closest friend.

I SECURED THE KITCHEN AND THE HOUSE and left to walk on the beach. I couldn't believe what Isabella had said. She knew how hard things were for me. Tears coursing down my cheeks, I headed for the water and plopped into the sand.

I stared out at the horizon, unable to calm myself down. I needed Jason.

Returning home to get the mini-van, I drove to the wharf, parked, and headed for Fishes Do Come True. All around me, happy people window-shopped, admired Christmas decorations, and smiled and laughed with one another. Everyone was in the holiday spirit. My bad mood had me feeling like Scrooge.

Jason was surprised to see me. "I thought you had a ton of stuff to bake."

"I do. And I'm stressed to the max. But something else has come up. I could use a bowl of clam chowder and a talk."

"Okay. Go take a seat and I'll be right there."

I settled into a booth.

Jason came out from the kitchen five minutes later with two clam chowder bread bowls and a couple of salads.

Once we'd both had a few bites, Jason said, "Understanding boyfriend ready to hear what's bothering you. It's not the break-in, is it? You don't seem scared so much as upset."

"It's Isabella. We had a huge fight."

"You two? That's surprising. You're as close as Flour and Sugar. What happened?"

I told him the whole story.

He put down his spoon. "Okay, do you want my take?"

"Yes. She was totally out of line, right?"

"I'd say you both were."

"*What*?" I almost yelled at him.

"You've got to admit that Brian and his partner are working hard."

"Maybe. But what about the things she said about my sensitivity?"

"She was out of line there, and I bet she's feeling badly about that right this second. You've told me how supportive she is normally."

"So was Adam until he wasn't."

"That's different. Isabella is squarely in your corner."

"Then why did she say what she did?"

He took my hand. "Think about why the argument started in the first place."

"She was telling me I shouldn't investigate."

"Right. And why is that? She's concerned about you, Kayla. She doesn't want to lose you. That's where this is all coming from. You can't blame her for that."

I opened my packet of oyster crackers with my teeth rather than answer.

"Okay, you're not ready to forgive her yet. So, this is what we're gonna do. We're going to finish our dinner and then I'm going to bring out some of the chocolate cake you brought in the other day, and we're going to eat it. Once we've done that, you will go see Isabella and make up."

"Wow, you're getting awfully bossy."

"Only because I know what's best for you in this one particular case. You know it, too, right?"

I couldn't agree with him yet. But I couldn't help myself; I smiled at him.

After cake and cocoa, I drove to the clubhouse restaurant and parked in the lot. I found Isabella clearing tables.

"Iz."

She pulled me into a hug. "Kayla. Will you ever forgive me? I'm so sorry I said those things. You know I respect that you're an HSP. I respect everything about you. But the dream felt so real. It freaked me out. Everything got out of hand."

"I know. The same thing happened with me when I said the things I did. I know Brian is trying. I'm just so upset about Trudy and Stanley. I *have* to do something, even if it puts me in danger. I promise I'm being careful."

"I shouldn't have told you what to do. It's not my place. I support you. I always will."

"Right back at you."

"Will you accept a gingerbread latte as an apology? Decaf, of course."

"That sounds perfect." I still had a lot to bake before the party, but making up with my best friend took priority.

We sat and enjoyed ourselves at a window table while looking out at the darkness. I told her about Flour's and Sugar's latest antics, and we talked about the holiday party the next day. We were excited about our costumes. We promised to get together then, and I left soon afterward.

I stayed up late baking and didn't get to bed until almost two.

THE NEXT MORNING, I CALLED MY MOM to firm up our plans for Christmas Eve and Christmas Day.

"We're so happy you're coming," Mom said. "It's been ages since we've seen each other."

"Yeah, the last time was when you came down in October for my birthday," I said. "I'm happy too."

"We'll have croissants and orange juice for Christmas Day breakfast while we open presents. Bob can make a fire. Then, if you're up for it, we'll walk on the hiking trail before our big turkey dinner. I'm making mashed potatoes, yams, and green beans, too, since we didn't get to have Thanksgiving together."

"That all sounds great."

"Good. I'm glad you called, sweetheart. I want to talk to you about something. The Chronicle ran a story yesterday about two murders in your community. What's that about? I'm worried."

I hadn't yet gotten around to telling my mother about the murders. Although we emailed a few times a week, I'd never found the right words. "Right. The murders. Well, the first victim was a very good friend of mine, Trudy Dillingham. You met her once, remember?"

"Yes, I thought the name sounded familiar. Why didn't you tell us?"

"I didn't want to worry you. It was bad, Mom. Trudy was eighty-nine. The police don't know why she was killed. She had no family left, so it wasn't a relative. She didn't have a caretaker or even a housekeeper. And she wasn't robbed."

"Did her past catch up with her?" This was my stepdad, Bob, who had come on the line.

"I've been wondering that myself. It might have been her past, yes. But she also did a few things shortly before her death that could have angered a person or two." I paused. It was hard to discuss what I'd discovered about Trudy. "She was blackmailing people."

"Blackmail," Mom said. "That's really something." She was so supportive that she didn't ask why I had a friend who would commit blackmail, something I'd been questioning as well.

"I know," I said. I decided not to tell them about the break-in yet. I knew it would only upset them. "Listen. A bride is coming to pick up her sugar cookies for her wedding shower. She'll be here any minute. I better go now."

"I'm sure the cookies are beautiful," my mom said. I thanked her and told her I'd whip up a peppermint cream pie for our Christmas dinner.

We all hung up just as I heard a tap at the door. It was my client, Leah Stegner, as expected. I retrieved the box of cookies, disarmed the security, and opened the door.

After we'd greeted each other, Leah peeked inside the box at the mermaid sugar cookies I'd frosted in yellows, blues, and greens. Her eyes lit up. "These are perfect, Kayla. Thank you." She took a check from the pocket of her jeans and gave it to me. I told her to enjoy her shower, and we said good-bye.

After I closed the door, I allowed myself a brief moment of daydreaming about my own bridal shower. A picnic on the beach, with seafood salads and tea sandwiches, would be nice.

Before I fell down the rabbit hole of planning my entire wedding to Jason, I shook myself out of the thoughts. I wanted to add shell-shaped cookies to the tops of the apple pies for the holiday party, and I needed to finish up some other things. I shut myself in the kitchen.

JASON ARRIVED WITH A WRAPPED PACKAGE an hour later, and he looked so handsome in a white cable knit sweater that the daydreams flared up again.

"Another present?" I asked.

"It's your official Christmas present. I couldn't wait until tomorrow."

We sat on the couch, and I undid the bow and removed the wrapping paper. I gasped as I held up a royal-blue blanket that was heavy in my hands.

"A weighted blanket? No way." I rubbed it across my face.

Jason smiled and nodded.

"I've always wanted one of these. Thank you so much." The pressure from the heaviness of a weighted blanket was believed to reduce anxiety and improve sleep. The therapist who'd suggested I was an HSP had recommended I buy one, but because the blankets were somewhat pricey, I'd never gotten around to it. It was the perfect gift. I hugged and kissed Jason in appreciation.

I rose to retrieve his Christmas present from under the tree—a gift basket stuffed with Chicago Cubs goodies.

He took a cap, a jersey, a few pens, and a cell phone case from the basket, the expression on his face giving me a clue of what he looked like as a boy.

"This is sweet of you, Kayla. Especially given your feelings for the Cubs."

"It's not that I have anything against them. I just want *my* teams to win. A's and Giants all the way."

Jason took off his sweater and put on the jersey. We drank cocoa and ate a few cookies. After that, we agreed it was time to go back to work, so we made a time to meet at the holiday party.

"Can't wait to see your costume," Jason said as he left.

"You, too, Mr. Claus. See you soon."

CHAPTER 15

I HAD BAKED GOODS TO DELIVER before the holiday party, both business-related and personal. I drove around Seaside Shores and downtown Oceanville dropping off cookies, pies, and cakes. Everyone was in a joyful mood, and I received many greetings and hugs, which, while sweet, was a little overstimulating.

I went back home to spend quiet time doing paperwork and logging the money I'd received into my software program. I'd collected a number of checks lately and made a note to deposit them after the holidays. The details of the work calmed me down and I was ready to begin the next part of my day.

Under the cats' watchful eyes, I began my transformation into an elf. I slipped on my long-sleeved green top and knee-length green skirt, then pulled on my red-and-white-striped tights. The tights bugged me a little bit, but I decided they would work for a few hours. Once I had everything on, I examined myself in the full-length mirror. I thought I looked pretty good. I completed the outfit by wrapping a red scarf around my neck and stepping into my pointy boots, which added an inch or so to my height of five foot two.

In the bathroom, I rubbed some blush into my pale cheeks. Lastly, I curled my shoulder-length blond hair before positioning the elf hat on my head. I loaded my desserts into the mini-van and left.

I arrived to the conference room at the clubhouse a few minutes later. Like the restaurant, the room overlooked the ocean. I allowed myself a moment of enjoying the glorious view.

After I tore myself away, I found the desserts table and began unloading my goodies. I made a few more trips to the mini-van to retrieve everything.

While I laid out my last few desserts, Isabella, dressed adorably as Ms. Claus, entered the room and ran over to me.

"Brian's coming in an hour," she said. "He was able to get off work after all."

"I'm so glad."

"Me too," she said. "This is going to be fun."

"You look *really* good," I told her. She was even more alluring in the conservative outfit than she'd been in the sexy costume. Her long dark curls spilled beguilingly from her hat, and her brown eyes looked bigger than ever.

"Thanks, Kayla. You're the cutest elf I've ever seen. I like the red on your cheeks. Did you use blush?"

"I did. Jason's bringing vats of clam chowder. I don't know where he is, though." I checked my watch. "We were supposed to meet right at four. Have you seen him?"

"No, but I'm sure he'll be here soon. Maybe it's taking longer than he expected to load the chowder into the catering van."

"Yeah, that's probably it."

THE ROOM FILLED UP QUICKLY WITH SANTAS, Mrs. Clauses, elves, and reindeer. I waved to Vicky and Angie when they walked in, Angie looking darling in reindeer ears, a furry costume, and a red nose. I saw Tristan, Dana Kim, and Nancy Dougherty too. But where was Jason?

Isabella, always at home at a party, was mingling. I went back to the floor-to-ceiling windows to look out again. While I watched a couple struggle to steer their kayak in the water, a person wearing a reindeer costume with a big head approached me.

"Hi, honey," the reindeer whispered.

"Jason?"

He nodded.

"What happened to your Santa costume?"

"Don't feel well. Sore throat. I don't want anyone to get sick. Better to have this on."

"Oh no. You were fine earlier."

"Came on suddenly."

"I'm sorry. You've been working so hard and your resistance was probably down."

He nodded again.

Something about him nagged at me. Okay, so he had a sore throat and didn't want to talk, and he was dressed as a big furry mammal besides, but something seemed off. Then I realized what it was. I wasn't picking up his usual appealing scent of citrus shampoo mixed with Ivory soap. He didn't seem to have a smell at all today. I tried to look him in the eyes, but the huge reindeer head covered his entire face. How could he even see?

"Why don't you take off the reindeer head for a minute?" I said.

"No, no. Don't want you to get sick," he said, still in a whisper. "Let's go outside and down to the water. It's noisy in here. I know you don't like that."

"Okay." I tried to shake off the feeling that something wasn't right. He was wearing a thick costume, so that's why I wasn't picking up a smell. And his voice sounded different because of the sore throat.

He took my hand and we walked outside and down the stairs to the beach. Even the way he held my hand felt different. I told myself it was the furry gloves he was wearing.

We walked for about a quarter of a mile without speaking. Then he stopped, turned to me, and playfully took my scarf. Just as I realized the truth of what was happening, he tightened the scarf around my neck. I tried to struggle out of his hold, but the scarf got tighter and tighter, and I couldn't gain purchase on his furry costume. I closed my eyes as my vision blurred.

The first thought that flashed through my mind was that I would die in a beautiful place, my favorite place in the world, near the ocean. The second thought was that this couldn't be Jason. Who was it?

"Where *is* it?" the reindeer man asked in a harsh whisper. He loosened his grip slightly so I could answer.

"Where is what?" I choked out.

In my haze, I heard a voice call, "Kayla!" Jason came running toward us. The reindeer man let go of me and tore off down the beach past Jason.

"The k-killer," I stuttered. I bent over and coughed a few times.

"My god, Kayla. Are you all right?" Jason asked, coming closer to me.

"Go after him!"

Jason sprinted after my attacker, and I followed, but it was no use. We were at a severe disadvantage because I couldn't catch my breath, I'd not removed my pointy shoes, and Jason had on his Santa costume and clunky boots. Finally, we gave up and stopped. I bent over again, and Jason placed his hand to my back.

"He tried to strangle me like he did Trudy and Stanley," I stammered, my throat burning with pain.

"We've got to get you to the hospital. We'll call the police on the way."

Jason put his arm around me, and we staggered toward the clubhouse parking lot. On the way, he called 911. After he hung up, we agreed my attacker had no doubt removed the costume by now, so the description he'd given the operator wouldn't be much help. And even if the attacker *hadn't* changed clothes, there were dozens of reindeer walking around today.

In response to my dejected look, Jason said, "Everything's going to be okay."

HOURS LATER, I WAS RELEASED from the hospital with only minor abrasions on my neck. While my voice was still somewhat hoarse, I felt extremely grateful to be alive. I had given my statement to Brian and told him my schedule for the next few days. He'd promised to arrange for an officer to drive by the cottage every few hours.

At home, Jason—still in his Santa suit—made tea, settled me on the couch, and covered me with the new weighted blanket. He brought the cats in from the bedroom, and they obliged by curling up next to me.

Jason sat at the other end of the couch and ran his hand through his hair. "If only I hadn't been so late. One of the tires on the catering van was flat and I had to change it."

We stared at each other as an idea hit us at the same time.

"That's some coincidence," I said.

"Or not." Jason took out his phone and called Brian to tell him.

Once Jason hung up with Brian, he turned to me. "Kayla, I insist that you let me spend the night. The couch is perfectly comfortable. I called Timothy when you were with the doctor. He's filling in for me tonight at the charity event."

I nodded. If he hadn't volunteered, I would have asked. We spent the next few hours watching TV and not speaking much. Finally, I got up to get sheets, pillows, and blankets for Jason and told him good-night.

IT TOOK ME A LONG TIME TO RELAX enough to fall asleep. Questions ran though my head: Who the heck was this guy who'd killed Trudy and

Stanley and now attacked me? What was he looking for? Why did he think I had it? What if Jason hadn't arrived when he had? I'd been fooled into thinking the reindeer man was Jason, but as I thought back on the incident, I realized my instincts had told me it wasn't him. Going forward, I would have to trust myself more or I'd never discover the murderer.

I WAS DISTRACTED AS JASON AND I ATE BREAKFAST the next morning, on Christmas Eve. Jason was still wearing his Santa costume, which under normal circumstances would have made me giggle. Something was bugging me, and I couldn't tease it out.

"Thinking about your ordeal?" Jason asked. He reached across the table and took my hand. "I'm so sorry, Kayla. I should have been there to protect you."

"It wasn't your fault. And, luckily, you *were* there at the right moment."

"I don't even want to think about what would have happened if I hadn't been." His eyes filled with sadness. "But it was a bad enough experience for you."

"It could have been worse. My voice is already better. I just have these abrasions and a turtleneck will cover them. I have to come up with a way to tell my parents when I see them and not have them freak out."

The sound of the cats' jangly ball interrupted our discussion. The ball landed near my feet, followed by Sugar.

"That's it," I said.

"What?"

"He knew I'm an HSP. Or at least that I don't like noise."

Jason thought for a moment. "Okay, that's good. Have you told anyone lately that you're an HSP?"

"Yes. Cliff, the gardener. I have to call Isabella." I jumped up from the table and went to find my phone.

Isabella was glad to hear from me. "Brian told me about the reindeer guy. I can't believe it. Are you all right? I knew something like this was going to happen. Remember my dream?"

"I'm fine. I promise. Does Brian have any ideas yet who it was?"

"I'm afraid not."

I couldn't sit back and do nothing. Now that two people had been murdered, two houses had been ransacked, and I'd been attacked, I needed to figure out who the killer was sooner rather than later. I explained to Isabella that I needed her help.

"Cliff will be at Jan Williams's next Thursday," I said. "Could you go over there and try to suss out what he was doing the day Trudy was killed? Jan says he called in sick, but he told me he was working."

"I can try. Won't he know why I'm asking?"

"Maybe you can come up with something brilliant as a cover."

"I accept that challenge."

This is why I loved her so much.

Jason and I finished breakfast and did the dishes. I changed into a turtleneck and checked the time.

"I better get going to my parents," I said. "Thanks for taking care of the cats." We'd decided the practical course of action was for him to continue bunking at the cottage so he'd be available to Sugar and Flour when he wasn't at work. I had the security measures in place and an officer would be driving by every few hours. I would never forgive myself if Reindeer Man came after Jason.

Just before I left, I remembered I'd promised to bring a pie for Christmas dinner. I'd forgotten all about it with everything that had gone on. Fortunately, I had sugar cookies in the freezer, which I packed up. I kissed the cats and Jason, loaded my carry-on and gifts into the mini-van, and began my drive north.

There wasn't much traffic, no doubt because of the holiday. I used the beginning of the trip to go over all I knew about Trudy and her death, but didn't end up with any answers. I was even having a few doubts about my prime suspect, Cliff the gardener. Would he really kill Trudy because she didn't cut him in on the pot sales? If he knew how to grow pot, couldn't he sell it himself? And, again, I had to remind myself that the money in her dresser drawer wasn't taken.

I gave up, turned on the radio, and listened to carols. My shoulders relaxed and the knot in my stomach loosened. The day before had been rough. When this was all over, I'd need several days of rest and recovery.

Mom and Bob came hurrying out of their townhouse when I drove up shortly before eleven. They ushered me inside, where Mom served a few of my sugar cookies with homemade cocoa.

Bob seemed off. He kept asking me to repeat myself and finally excused himself to work in the garage.

After he left, I looked at Mom. "What's up with him? He's not making any jokes. And he hasn't called you Lady Di once." Early on in their relationship, Mom, who'd been named after the Roman goddess Diana, had told Bob she was a fan of the British royalty. From that point forward, he often called her "Lady Di" after the late princess.

"Long story," Mom said.

"I'm not going anywhere."

Mom twirled her earring with her thumb and forefinger. Her brown hair, which she already wore short, looked like it had recently been cut. "He's been playing the stock market. Without my knowledge. And he lost money."

I blinked at least five times. "What?"

"Kayla, do I really need to say it again?"

"No. I just can't . . . This is so hard to believe. He's always been conservative with money. What happened?"

"He wants to take a cruise in Europe. It's expensive."

"He lost a lot?"

"A fairly good sum."

I played with the cookie crumbs on my plate. "Did you have a fight about it?"

"Yes. It's mostly blown over. I just wish he'd told me."

Bob came back into the room, so we stopped talking. He went past us and up the stairs. His shoulders were stooped, making him look shorter than his six-three frame.

"Listen, darling," Mom said as soon as Bob was out of earshot, "Mona next door invited us over tonight for a small party. We weren't going to go, but I think it could be good for Bob. Why don't you come too?"

"Honestly, I'm exhausted from the road trip. I think I'll just read tonight."

"Okay. We won't be home late."

ONCE MOM AND BOB LEFT FOR THE PARTY, I went looking for our cat. Callie, a calico with sweet amber eyes and a glossy coat, was eighteen and going strong. I found her lying on the couch and picked her up to take her with me to the guest room. Callie was an agreeable sort, and she immediately cuddled up next to me in bed.

I'd texted Jason when I arrived and he texted back while I was reading to wish me a happy Christmas. I responded with a thank you and a similar greeting.

Before going to sleep, I looked out the window to the San Francisco Bay. The Bay Lights, the world's largest light art installation, sparkled along the San Francisco-Oakland Bay Bridge. I knew how much Mom and Bob appreciated this beautiful view, which rivaled my own of Oceanville Bay. Bob had grown up in landlocked Minnesota and was an adult before he saw the ocean. He loved living in the Bay Area.

Mom met Bob at a party a year after she and my dad divorced. They married eleven months later. Dad had moved to Florida following the divorce, so Bob became a substitute father for me. I loved him with all my heart. He was one of the kindest, most honest people I knew. I couldn't believe he had kept a financial decision from my mom.

As I drifted off to sleep, I wondered: Did everyone have secrets?

CHRISTMAS DAY DAWNED BRIGHT AND SUNNY. Mom and I went for a walk in the hills near the townhouse after the three of us exchanged presents and ate breakfast. Bob had declined our invitation to go with us.

I put on my clip-ons and took off the cardigan I wore over my turtleneck. I'd chosen the turtleneck again to cover the abrasions on my throat, but I'd decided to tell Mom about the attempted strangling. I had to find the right moment.

"How's it going with Bob after the party last night?" I asked.

"Marriage is a lot of work," Mom said, adjusting the light-blue scarf I'd given her. After all the trouble with the scarves, I was happy she liked it as much as she did.

"That's your answer? Doesn't sound good."

"It'll be fine. You have to give each other space after a disagreement. Allow each other to calm down."

"And did that happen?"

"Yes. He feels terribly. Now it's up to me to soothe him for a mistake I'm mad about. Marriage is not only hard but strange." She laughed.

"Do you recommend it?" I asked, curious. "The first wasn't so good."

"The first one was a disaster, yes, but without it I wouldn't have had you, which was the best thing that's ever happened to me." She turned and smiled at me.

"It worked out pretty well for me too," I said.

"I'm glad you feel that way. Back to your question. On balance, the second marriage is light years better. I think it's best to get married when you're a little older."

"When you're thirty-five, like I am, you mean?"

"I didn't say that. You won't get any pressure from me."

"Even though you always coo over baby clothes at stores, and I'm your only bet?"

"I would never want you to have children unless it was your idea. I want you to do what makes you happy. Period."

"Thanks. I don't know about kids, but there actually is a guy."

She bent to the trail to pick up a stone in the shape of a heart. "Interesting I found this at that exact second." She handed it to me.

I turned the stone over in my palm. "He's great. He owns a successful restaurant." I hesitated. "I just . . ."

"You're worried that it will end up like Adam?"

"I am." A bird in the tree near us sang out and we both looked up at it.

"Do you remember Carl Hillman?" Mom asked.

I tilted my head. "Yeah. That's the guy you dated before you met Bob, right?"

"I thought we could build a life together. He cheated on me."

I stared at her in surprise. "You never told me that. You just said it didn't work out."

"It wasn't your problem and you were a teenager. The point is, when you've been hurt badly, you expect it to happen again."

I looked into her eyes. "But?"

"Not all men are the same. Bob is a very good man."

"So is Jason. He's sweet to me. He's funny and smart. He's supportive of my sensitivity and my baking. And he makes excellent clam chowder."

Mom chuckled. "Sounds like a keeper. You could have brought him, you know."

"It was too soon. Maybe we can arrange for you and Bob to come down and see us. You can meet the cats in person, now that you've seen countless pictures of them."

She squeezed my arm. "We'd love that."

"Mom, Jason might be the guy."

"I'm glad. But, remember, no pressure from me."

"I know."

"Now what about this awful business? Not only your friend, but someone else too?"

"Yes. Stanley. He was an elderly friend of Trudy's." I took a deep breath. "There's something else, Mom, that I haven't told you."

"Oh?"

"I don't want you to worry, but the murderer came after me."

Mom stopped short. "What did you just say?"

"First, my house was broken into. Nothing was taken, though. Then, at the holiday party, he tried to strangle me." I pulled my sweater out from my neck to show her the abrasions.

She gasped. "Kayla, darling. That's the most horrible thing I've ever heard. Why would he go after *you*?"

We started walking again as I formulated my response.

"Well, I've been doing a little investigating on my own. That might be a reason, but it's not the only one. He wants something of Trudy's that he believes I have. I don't know what that thing is, though. And I've been trying to work out who the guy is, but I can't do it. It's driving me nuts."

Mom stopped and put her arm to mine. "I don't like this one bit, Kayla. You're obviously in danger. What about the police, for heaven's sake? Isn't this *their* job?"

"They're trying but haven't made any headway. I feel I have an advantage over them because of my friendship with Trudy, even though she wasn't the person I thought she was. Don't worry, Mom. Jason will stay with me. And the police are driving by the cottage every few hours. I'm safe."

"Of course it's your decision," Mom said as we picked up our pace again, "but why don't you stay here with us until it's all over?"

"Thank you. I appreciate that. But I have to see this through. Trudy was special to me. Poor Stanley was ninety-one. They must both have been so scared."

Mom nodded thoughtfully. "Yes."

"I promised myself I'd find the killer, Mom. Tell me you understand."

Mom was quiet for a moment. "All right, then. Who's your top suspect?"

I was grateful she wasn't pressuring me to give up. "I don't know. Everyone has an alibi. Well, there is one person who lied about his alibi. Isabella's going to check on it for me. But I'm having doubts about him."

We'd reached the tree where we usually turned around. Without talking about it, we circled the maple. I looked up at the tree, now bare of leaves. Without them, the maple looked vulnerable and alone. Sometimes I felt like that, especially now given what had happened in my quiet little corner of the world.

"I told you about the blackmail," I said. "Trudy was cheating at bingo and selling pot too. She obviously needed money, but why?"

"Maybe she was also being blackmailed?"

"That's an interesting idea. About something from her past, possibly. And she was killed because she couldn't come up with enough money?"

Mom considered. "Do you remember how much you liked puzzles when you were little?"

"Yes."

"Well, as you know, we didn't know about HSPs back then. You tended to get agitated. But if I placed a puzzle book in front of you, you immediately calmed down and became completely absorbed."

"It's interesting you should bring this up. I made a logic grid to help me figure out the killer. It hasn't worked so far, though."

"You were good, Kayla. You didn't give up until you'd solved them all. I've no doubt you're going to solve this."

"I hope so. Trudy meant a lot to me."

"I wish I'd had a chance to get to know her."

"Me too."

A jogger went by, and we all said "hello" and "Merry Christmas."

Mom and I took a few steps without speaking. Then she checked her watch. "Let's get a move on. We'll have cocoa when we get home. Sing a few carols. Bob is going to dance for us. Then I'll put the turkey in and make the rest of our dinner."

I laughed. "Bob? Dance?"

"Yes, he's been practicing a little routine for us. You'll like it, I think."

"Now *that* I've got to see."

THE PROMISED DANCE, SET TO THE TUNE OF "Santa Claus is Coming to Town," was well worth seeing. We had a lovely Christmas Day and dinner. Best of all, my mother and Bob seemed to be doing better. Bob held Mom's hand at dinner and they smiled at each other often. He called her Lady Di at least twice, so I knew things were back to normal. When it was time to go home the next morning, a melancholy settled over me, but I knew we would visit again soon. I was looking forward to seeing Jason and the cats.

CHAPTER 16

THE AFTERNOON AFTER CHRISTMAS, Jason put in an appearance at the restaurant and I stayed home to read on the couch with the weighted blanket covering me. The cats batted around their jangly ball on the floor next to me, looking up periodically for my approval. All was right with the world when someone came to the door. I'd gotten over my tendency to have a heart attack whenever anyone knocked, and without thinking it through, I disabled the alarm, undid the locks, and swung open the door.

Standing on the porch was a man in a black ski mask. I tried to slam the door in his face, but he caught it and held it open. He pushed me back into the living room with hands covered by thick black gloves. Out of the corner of my eye, I saw Flour and Sugar take refuge underneath the couch.

"You have it, don't you?" he whispered. It was the reindeer man!

"I don't know what you mean. I'm telling you, I don't have anything." I backed up.

He advanced toward me and I backed up again, wracking my brain for something to hit him with. On TV, I'd seen people hit by lamps, but the only lighting nearby was a heavy floor lamp I didn't think I could maneuver.

"Where *is* it?" my attacker said.

"I don't know, I swear. I don't know what you want."

I backed up farther until I was standing on the fireplace hearth.

"Tell me!"

And then his hands were around my neck.

A paw came out from underneath the couch and swatted at the jangly ball. The toy rolled across the room. My attacker was so surprised that he let go of me just enough so I could wrench myself free. Frantic, I took the closest thing to me, which was Tristan's painting, and crushed it over his head. I ran to the dining room table, tossed aside the dome from the apple pie I'd intended for Jason and me to share that evening, and threw the dessert into his face. While he sputtered, I grabbed my messenger bag from the table and tore outside.

I'd barely gotten into the mini-van and locked it before he came running outside. I switched on the ignition and zoomed down the driveway. As I turned onto Sea Lion Drive, my phone rang. Jason.

"He's here. He's after me. Help!"

"I'll call the police."

IT WAS DÉJÀ VU ALL OVER AGAIN. Brian and Lisa arrived to take my statement while officers spread out to look for my attacker. The crime scene investigators started their work of trying to recover DNA. As for me, I tried to come to terms with what had become of my life.

While the forensics team went through the cottage, Jason took me for a walk. I couldn't stop shaking. Jason kept his arm securely around my waist and didn't pressure me to speak.

MUCH LATER, I LOOKED AT THE BLANK SPACE where my beautiful work of art had been, then down to the floor to the remnants of the painting. I burst into tears.

"Oh, honey," Jason said, coming over to hug me. "He'll paint you another one, I'm sure."

"Why did I have to use the painting? Why, why, why?"

"You were acting on instinct. And it was good instinct. That and the pie let you escape. How many paintings can say that?"

I smiled. "Or pies? I always knew baking would save me. I just wish the police had caught him."

"Since he was on foot, he probably removed the mask and joined the crowds on the walking path when he realized he couldn't get you."

I sighed. "It's the second time he escaped."

"I know, but it's going to be all right, Kayla. I doubt he'll try again. I think I better continue staying with you, just in case."

"Okay. Knowing you'll be here makes me feel better. Thanks."

Isabella called a few minutes later. Brian had told her what had happened. I promised her I was fine and let her know Jason was staying with me. We agreed to see each other soon.

JASON AND I SPENT THE NEXT FEW DAYS COHABITATING. Now that it was the week between Christmas and New Year's, there was a lull in business at Fishes Do Come True. Although Jason had to go to work every so often, he was able to stay with me quite a bit. I, too, didn't have much on my schedule. We went for walks, talked a lot, and made a few desserts for ourselves. Gradually, my nerves settled down and I felt more like myself. On Wednesday night, we met up with Paula and went to the movies. Afterward, she came to the cottage to meet Sugar and Flour.

On Thursday evening, Isabella came over, bursting with news. She didn't even want to sit down until she'd told me.

"I saw Cliff," she said.

Of course. I'd tasked her with following up with Cliff, the gardener. Was he the one who'd attacked me at the party and at my house? Now that I thought about it, my attacker did have the same build as Cliff. Although his physique had been disguised by the reindeer suit on the day of the holiday party, I'd gotten a good look at his form when he barged into my house.

"It's true," Isabella went on. "He called in sick on November fourth. He wasn't murdering Trudy, though."

"What, then?"

"He's an alcoholic and he's been struggling lately. He's been going to a bunch of AA meetings, sometimes more than one a day. I checked on the internet for the times and places he mentioned and they match up. He was at a meeting when Trudy was killed."

I let a few beats go by. "That's it?"

"Yes. I'm afraid so."

"I'll put it on my grid. Isabella, how in the world did you get the information?"

She shot me a Cheshire Cat smile. "I asked him."

"And he told you?"

She shrugged.

"You're a great investigator, Iz, you know that? Speaking of which, what's the news from Brian? Has he given you any inside information lately?"

"No, and he wants you to back off. He's more afraid than ever that you're going to get hurt. Which you have been. He didn't believe for a second that you'd ever stopped investigating."

"Oh boy."

I opened the kitchen door and went in. I came back with a few cookies, and Isabella and I curled up with the cats on the couch.

"Oh my gosh," I said. "I forgot to give you your present."

I went over to the tree and came back with an envelope with her name on it.

She tore open the flap and took out the gift card I'd made. I'd drawn the cats playing with the ornaments on the Christmas tree, not especially well. My skills with desserts didn't translate to other artistic endeavors. I'd written the pertinent details for the gift card below the drawing.

"It's admission to an online LSAT prep course," I explained.

Isabella didn't say anything, and I realized I'd made a mistake. She'd been studying on her own for the LSAT and probably felt she was doing fine. I'd no doubt insulted her.

"Iz, I know you're doing great on your own. I—"

Before I could finish, she grabbed me and hugged me.

"This is the best gift I've ever gotten," she said, a few tears gathering in her eyes. "I've had such a hard time doing it by myself. I was beginning to think I'd never get into law school. I envisioned my dreams crumbling all around me."

I relaxed. "Oh good. I'm so glad."

She glanced at the gift card again. "This is such a thoughtful present. Thank you, Kayla. Really."

"You're very welcome."

"Your present hasn't arrived yet. There was a shipping delay. I'll get it to you ASAP."

"No worries."

We went back to eating cookies.

"Where's Jason?" Isabella asked in between bites.

"At the restaurant. He'll be back soon."

"Good. I'm glad he's staying with you."

I nodded. "I was so hoping it was Cliff. I'd told him I'm sensitive to noise."

Isabella turned to me and took my hands. "I know. But this has to stop now. Please. You're going to get yourself killed. Will you leave it up to Brian and Lisa?"

I had to face the facts. I didn't know who the killer was, but he sure knew me. One of these days, he might actually succeed in strangling me.

"Yes. I'm done," I said.

I meant it at the moment. Then Isabella went missing on New Year's Eve.

CHAPTER 17

B RIAN WAS BESIDE HIMSELF. He paced around the cottage, muttering under his breath, while I sat on the couch fiddling with my birthstone ring. Flour and Sugar, equally excited and confused, followed Brian around. I desperately wanted to give him reassurance but I wasn't able to do it. I was beside myself too.

"When's the last time you saw her? This is important, Kayla."

"I saw her at the clubhouse," I said. "We had coffee this morning. Around ten."

"You didn't hear from her after that?"

"No. I tried to call her later—a few times—around two thirty. Her voice mail came on right away every time."

"Vincent said she left work at noon. She was due back at two to set up for the New Year's Eve dinner. She didn't show. I went inside her house, and I don't think she's been there, but it's impossible to tell."

I looked at him quickly. He had a key? That was news.

Brian ran his hand across his chin, obviously distressed. It was inappropriate given the circumstances, but my spirits lifted. This guy cared about Isabella. I couldn't wait to tell her. Well, I couldn't wait to see her either.

"Brian, tell me the truth. Do you think the killer has her? Does he think she knows something? Like where 'it' is? Whatever that is? Does he think I told her?" The idea was a stab to my heart. I knew this was all my fault.

He stared back at me with haunted eyes. "I think it's possible, and we're no closer to knowing who the killer is."

I had to agree with that, but I didn't say anything. I wasn't supposed to be involved.

Brian left soon afterward, urging me to stay at home with the alarm on and all my locks secured. He also told me to let him know immediately if Isabella called.

The cats prowled around the room, unable to settle.

"Sit with me, okay?" I said to them.

They obliged by jumping up next to me. We were all just waiting for something to happen.

EXCEPT I WASN'T VERY GOOD AT WAITING, especially when my best friend's life might be at stake. After ten minutes, I rose from the couch and paced around the room like Brian had. Trying to tamp down my dual emotions of fear and guilt, I found my logic grid and reviewed everything I knew.

I knew a man had attacked me, a man of a particular stature. I looked over the list of male suspects who were around six feet tall with a medium build, coming up with Cliff the gardener, Mayor Lars Chapman, the librarian Topher Fremont, and Trudy's neighbor Austin Williams. Trudy hadn't cut Cliff in on her pot sales, but he'd been at an AA meeting at the time of her death. The mayor had been at a reelection party when Trudy was killed, a party I knew had taken place because I'd read about it in the community newsletter.

I'd never double-checked Topher Fremont's alibi of being at the library. Believing at the time that Trudy's observatory would block his and his wife's view, maybe he'd killed her to stop the project in its tracks. I decided his build was more muscular than my attacker's, so that let him out. Austin Williams had been eating lunch and flirting with Isabella, so it wasn't him either. What was I missing? Did Trudy have another secret I had yet to uncover? Someone else she was blackmailing, for example?

I found the scrapbook Eileen had brought me, hoping it held some clue to Trudy's life I'd missed the first time. I returned to the couch. Flour moved onto my lap and I stroked her as I paged through the book. Nothing jumped out at me.

The scrapbook slipped from my hands and fell to the floor. A newspaper article floated out. It must have been lodged behind one of the photos.

The article detailed an armed robbery at a jewelry store in downtown Oceanville in the 1980s. The thieves, whom the paper billed a "Modern Day Bonnie and Clyde," were believed to be a man and a woman, though they were heavily disguised. A number of expensive jewels, including diamonds, were stolen. The police had no leads.

In that moment, it all came together.

I CALLED EILEEN AND CONFIRMED what I suspected. The mayor had helped clean out Trudy's house.

"I thought it was nice that he came to help out," Eileen said. "He must have read about it in the newsletter."

"Was he ever off on his own?"

"Let me think. Yes, I suppose he was. Why?"

"I'll explain another time. I have to go. Thanks."

I CALLED BRIAN AND TOLD HIM what I thought. He didn't find my evidence compelling.

"Why would he want the jewels this many years later? And kill someone he presumably cared about? Why did he say 'it' instead of 'they'?"

I had to admit I didn't know the answers to any of those questions.

Brian continued, "Do you know his whereabouts at the times of the murders?"

I mumbled that while I didn't know where he was at the time of Stanley's murder, Lars had been at a reelection party when Trudy was killed. Brian's sigh traveled down the phone line.

"Even if you're right and he has Isabella at his house, I can't get in without a search warrant," he said.

"But—"

"Look, Kayla, because I want to find Isabella as much as you do, I'll go over and see if he'll give me consent to go inside. If he says no, there's nothing I can do except get a warrant. Hold tight."

What seemed like an hour later, but was probably only fifteen minutes, Brian called back.

"No answer," he said. "The curtains were drawn so I couldn't look through the windows. I'll see if I can get a search warrant. It'll take time."

Time is what I didn't have. I had to save Isabella before the mayor hurt her. I needed to get in, and I knew exactly how.

DECIDING TO GO ON FOOT so I could retreat quickly if necessary, I left the cottage. I called Jason, who had gone to work shortly before Brian arrived, deciding it was prudent to tell *someone* what I was doing. He didn't answer, so I left a message.

I hurried along the coastal walk. I glanced out to the ocean and saw the waves coming in harder than usual. Overhead, clouds were gathering into ominous formations. I hadn't brought a raincoat or umbrella.

No one was around. Everyone must be inside, escaping the inclement weather and preparing for New Year's Eve.

A lump formed in my throat. Everything was going to heck. This was how I was spending New Year's Eve? Jason and I had planned to order a pizza for dinner and stay up to midnight. We should be looking out to the ocean, having playtime with the cats, and stuffing ourselves. Instead, I was trying to save my best friend from a maniacal killer.

I arrived at the mayor's house a few minutes later and saw neither of the BMWs in the circular driveway. I sneaked around to the side of the house and went through the gate into the patio. I listened as closely as I could but didn't hear any signs of life.

On the day I brought Beverly the lemon cake, I'd seen the cat flap cut into the sliding glass door. I extended my arm through the flap as I'd read burglars had been doing in Shelltown. After only a couple of tries, I managed to reach up and unlock the door.

I stepped inside and the alarm blared. I sprinted through to the front of the house and disarmed it, remembering the code Beverly had used. She had been so flustered by the alarm sounding after she'd put in the wrong code that she didn't think to hide the *right* code from me.

I padded through the house. It definitely seemed unoccupied. I kept going, scared out of my mind, but at least relieved that the Chapmans weren't there.

Then I heard a rustling on the stairs.

THE RUSTLING TURNED OUT TO BE JAKE, the Chapmans' tuxedo cat. He came down the stairs to me and rubbed against my legs.

"Sorry, sweetheart, no time."

I went past him up the stairs. I traveled room by room until I came upon one that was locked from the outside.

I pounded on the door. "Iz, are you in there?"

A weak voice called back, "Kayla, I'm here. Help!"

One of the rooms I'd looked in was an office with a rolltop desk. I told Isabella I'd be right back and tore down the hallway to the office. Trembling with apprehension, I rifled through the drawers until I found a keyring. I prayed there would be a spare key for the locked room. My hands were shaking so badly that I dropped the keyring on the desk, making an unholy noise. I picked it up and ran back to Isabella's prison. I tried key after key. Nothing. Until the last one, which worked.

Isabella sat with her arms around her knees in a corner, her eyes red and her face pale. I rushed over to her.

"Iz, honey, are you okay?"

"I think so. I need water."

"Okay." I rushed to the nearest bathroom, filled a glass that had held a toothbrush, and returned to her.

She drank the entire glass quickly. "Thank you."

"I'm so sorry about this. How did he get you?"

"It's both of them. They found me walking home from work. They offered me a ride, and then took me here instead of home. They're looking for diamonds, Kayla. *Diamonds.* They think you told me where they are. To buy time, I said I wasn't sure where they were, but they might be in the fake rock at Trudy's house or her locker at the senior center. Lars went to one place and Beverly to the other. I don't know how they'll get access to the locker, but they seem resourceful."

"We better go. They could come back any second." I helped her to her feet.

Unfortunately, our way out of the room was blocked. Beverly stood in the doorway.

BEVERLY SAID, "YOU'VE BEEN A VERY BAD GIRL, ISABELLA. They weren't in either place. And we never said you were allowed visitors."

Lars brushed past her into the room. He rummaged around in my pockets, took my phone, and pushed me, then Isabella, down into the corner. Meanwhile, Beverly removed a gun from her jacket pocket and directed it at us.

Lars did a double take. "Where did you get that?"

"At your girlfriend's house. *It* was easy to find. Don't you recognize it? From that little escapade you never told me about?"

"What are you going to do with it?" Lars asked.

I blinked my eyes a few times. There was a lot here to unpack. Trudy had a gun? Another secret? More to the point, why had Beverly taken the reins of this operation? Was *she* the killer? But my attacker had been male. Had they split the killing and attacking duties? What skillful stranglers they were. They must have taken the same online course. Now Beverly had stepped it up by bringing a gun into the mix. What a charming couple.

Beverly's eyes flitted over me while all this went through my mind. "We kill them, of course," she said.

Isabella let out a cry and I looked to her in alarm.

"Then we'll *never* get them," Lars protested.

Beverly pointed the gun at me. "Show some respect. Tell your mayor where they are RIGHT THIS SECOND."

I knew now they were referring to the diamonds stolen in the robbery. "I know you and Trudy robbed the jewelry store," I said to Lars.

"Well, congratulations," Beverly said. "But you haven't told us anything yet. One of you should answer soon or the other of you will be dead."

"Honestly, I have no idea," I said. "And Isabella doesn't either."

"That's right. I don't," Isabella said.

"Really?" Beverly turned to Isabella. "Then your friend the baker is dead." She aimed the gun at my head. I wished I'd had time to say good-bye to Jason. And the cats.

"Okay, okay," Isabella said. "Kayla does have them. She hid them at her house." She looked at me pleadingly for backup.

"That's right," I said, picking up the lie. "This is the truth, okay? Trudy put them in a special place that only I knew about. She wanted me to have them when she died. She knew I could use the money for a new kitchen. So, after I found her and was waiting for the ambulance and police, I went and got them. I put them in the pocket of my jeans. Later, I stashed them inside the mouth of the decorative frog on my front porch."

Lars looked skeptical. "You're talking about the rin . . . I mean, why should we believe you?"

"Because I'm done pretending. I don't care anymore. You can have them and no one has to know. Just let us go."

"That's funny," Beverly said. "I'll go and see if you're finally telling the truth." She handed the gun to Lars and left.

Now we had only one of them to contend with. Unfortunately, while there was only one person, there was still one gun.

"Your wife killed Trudy?" I asked Lars. "How do you feel about that?"

Lars looked pained. "Beverly said it was self-defense. Trudy attacked her. She went crazy, Bev said."

"I seriously doubt that." This time, I was sure about one part of Trudy's character. She would never try to kill someone. "I think your wife knew exactly what she was doing and *wanted* to kill her. You must be upset about that. You loved Trudy."

He began to weep, and I wondered if I could rush him and knock the gun out of his hand.

"Did she say the same thing about Stanley?" I asked, opting to push more of his buttons to see if he'd let down his guard further. "They both had a good thirty years on her. I don't see how they could have been much of a threat."

This made Lars sob even more. He seemed awfully emotional. I could use that.

"Come on, Lars. Don't make this any worse than it is. I don't think you ever wanted anyone to get hurt. I know you wouldn't have killed me when it came down to it. Let us go."

"I can't. You both know too much." He took a handkerchief from his pocket and wiped his eyes.

Outside of the room, a phone buzzed.

"I'm expecting an important call," he said, apparently under the impression that he could continue on with his mayoral duties as though nothing had happened. "Don't try anything." He left the room and locked the door.

Isabella turned to me. "How do we get out of here?" she whispered. "We don't have a phone. Lars took mine and threw it into the ocean."

"Maybe if we keep him talking, he'll loosen up and won't be holding the gun as tightly. Then we can rush him and run out the door. I think it's our only chance. Iz, do you know what the TAC is?"

"The what?"

"The T-A-C."

"Oh. You mean the Theresa Alden Center? It's just another term for the senior center. Why are you talking about this now?"

"In Seaside Shores?"

"Yes. Why?"

"The party that Trudy told me about on the phone the day she died. It was the reelection party for Lars. I bet Trudy saw Beverly at the center, and for some reason, they went back to Trudy's house together. I couldn't work out how Beverly could have killed Trudy when she supposedly had an alibi. Lars himself would have been missed if he wasn't at his own party, but a short absence on her part wouldn't have been questioned. It's a short walk from the center to Trudy's house. I wish I'd figured that out sooner. I wish I'd figured *all* of this out sooner."

"He's coming."

Once Lars was back in the room, and the gun was directed at us again, I said, "How did you meet Trudy, anyway?"

"Look, this isn't a dinner party."

"We have nothing else to do, right?"

"I met her at an astronomy lecture. She was the most beautiful thing I'd ever seen. Her eyes were magical. Like emeralds."

Next, he'd be saying her lips were like rubies. He had it bad.

He went on to tell us about their first conversation. He had a dreamy look on his face, and I became more confident Isabella and I could overtake him.

Before we had time to put the plan forward, Beverly came back. She took the gun from Lars and pointed it at Isabella's head. This was the bad news. The better news was I'd worked something out that might help us.

"I knew I couldn't trust you two," Beverly said. "Nothing."

"You didn't find the ring?" I said. "That's what you were about to say a while ago, wasn't it, Lars? I didn't understand why you kept asking where 'it' was instead of 'they.' Now I know."

Both Lars and Beverly stared at me.

"Ring?" Beverly asked. She turned to Lars. "Did you have the diamonds made into a *ring* for her?"

"No."

"A diamond ring as in an *engagement* ring? Did you *propose*?"

"No, no, no."

"I don't believe you. You . . . you bas—"

"Beverly, please."

"I'm glad I killed her, then."

"What are you saying? You killed her on purpose?"

"Yes."

Lars sank to the floor. "I can't believe it. Because of the affair? I thought . . . I thought you forgave me."

Beverly's face was tight. She appeared completely unmoved by Lars's pain. "I did forgive you for that. When she told me about the robbery, I forgave you for that too. What I couldn't forgive is that you gave *her* the diamonds." Beverly held up her left hand to display her wedding band and amethyst engagement ring. "Remember this? You couldn't afford a diamond when you proposed to me and you refused to take money from your family. You always promised to give me one to replace this crummy thing, but you never did. Those diamonds should have been mine. Why should she have your heart *and* the diamonds? Little did I know you'd made them into an engagement ring. For your mistress instead of your wife."

Lars giving Trudy a diamond ring was a betrayal for sure, but did no one grasp the fact that the diamonds weren't for anyone to give? They'd been stolen. Beverly seemed unfazed by the news that Lars had robbed a jewelry store. She was more concerned he hadn't given her the diamonds. It was hard to wrap my head around this couple and their values.

Meanwhile, Beverly had dropped her arm and the gun was no longer pointed at Isabella's head. This could be our chance to escape. I tried to communicate telepathically to Isabella that we should be ready to run at the earliest opportunity. I looked over at her and raised my eyebrows. She gave me a slight nod.

Lars covered his face with his hands. He whispered, "You didn't have to kill her."

Beverly straightened her shoulders, her mouth a grim line. "She wouldn't say where the diamonds were. It was her fault for admitting there were jewels left over that the two of you didn't sell."

"Did you kill the old guy on purpose too?" Lars squeaked out.

"He was out walking his dog that afternoon and saw me with Trudy. I threatened him not to tell anyone, but he was a loose end I had to tie up eventually."

"Oh, Beverly."

"Could you focus, please? I want those diamonds. Your wife deserves those diamonds. Do something."

She now pointed the gun at *him*.

The loud doorbell sounded, startling all of us.

I took the opportunity to rise, grab Isabella's hand, pull her up, and push past Lars and Beverly, all in one swift movement. Isabella and I ran down the stairs, and I flung open the front door. Brian and two policemen rushed in.

"They're upstairs!" I cried. "Hurry. Beverly might shoot Lars!"

CHAPTER 18

B RIAN AND THE POLICEMEN got to Lars and Beverly before any harm could befall the mayor. The Chapmans were taken into custody and, god willing, they would be locked up for a long time. I personally never wanted to see either one again. The only member of the Chapman household I'd liked was Jake the tuxedo cat. I hoped he'd have a new home soon—that wasn't mine. I didn't think I could take on *another* pet.

I SLEPT FOR A GOOD TWELVE HOURS and felt okay in the morning, but I knew it would take time to come to terms with what Isabella and I had been through. Jason suggested I talk to a therapist, and I was considering it.

That evening, Jason and I ate tacos on the couch and cuddled up together. But the cats' bowls of dry food were empty, and they meowed at me indignantly.

"Would you mind feeding them more Meow Munchables?" I asked Jason. "I'm so comfortable. I don't want to get up."

"So it begins," he said.

"What begins?"

"My life of waiting on you hand and foot."

"Sounds good to me, although technically, you're waiting on them and not me."

"Semantics," he said, and we laughed.

He got up and went inside the kitchen. When he didn't come back right away, I called, "Jason?"

He came out of the kitchen holding an empty bag of Meow Munchables and a lined piece of paper.

"What's going on?" I asked. I went over to him. "What's that paper? Where did it come from?"

"It was at the bottom of the bag."

I took the empty bag from him. "Where did you find this bag?"

"In the cupboard. The container on the counter was empty, so I filled it."

"Oh right. I'd forgotten all about this bag. The one I've been using ran out and I meant to replace it, but Isabella went missing. This bag came with Sugar. I used it for a while. Then Flour arrived with a new bag and I started using that one instead."

"Kayla, never mind about the food. Take a look at this. It's a letter from Trudy."

I hastily fed the cats and we went back to the couch. I read the letter out loud.

Dearest Kayla,

If you're reading this, it means what I feared has happened. I am dead. Not just dead but murdered. I know I have a lot to explain.

When I was a young woman, I believed the world was mine for the taking. I did things I regret. I hurt people. I stole things. If I had it all to do over, there are many, many things I would do differently.

I wish I could chalk it up to the foolishness of youth, but my misdeeds went on way past the time when I should have known better. In fact, they have continued to this day, and I must consider that any of the people I've wronged could decide to exact revenge. Still, I will tell you the most likely suspect.

In my early fifties, I fell in love with a married man—Lars Chapman. You know him as the mayor of Oceanville. We began an affair. It was exciting and dangerous, and I was always looking for ways to make things even more thrilling for us. I convinced him to rob a jewelry store with me. I'd gotten a taste for crime when I was younger, and I wanted to try something more difficult. I knew a lot of people back then and I was able to obtain a gun.

Lars and I held up the store and stole expensive jewels. Most of them we were able to sell, but Lars kept some diamonds and had them made into a ring for me. He would never leave Beverly because they had children. The ring was his way of showing he would have married me if he could.

The ring was our secret, and I wore it only in the privacy of my own home. One day, my ex, Oscar Lancaster, paid me an unexpected visit. I didn't think to remove the ring, and he pressed me to explain where it had come from. I told him about the robbery and the ring's provenance.

It felt good to confess to someone, but it was a grave error. Oscar was livid that I'd broken up with him to get involved with someone who would commit armed robbery. Someone who was married, besides. Oscar fancied himself a moral person despite helping me vandalize the governor's office when we were together.

When Lars ran for mayor the first time—this was in the early 2000s— he was up against Oscar's son. Lars beat Weston easily, enraging Oscar further. Shortly after the election, he came to see me. He said that the citizens of Oceanville deserved to know their newly-elected mayor had been involved in an armed robbery. Especially because Lars had run his campaign as a law and order candidate.

By then, my affair with Lars was over . . . I'd finally broken it off. We'd parted before whenever the guilt got to us but always ended up together again. This time, it was for good. But I still loved him, Kayla. I loved him dearly. The statute of limitations on the robbery had run out, but the news could ruin him. I couldn't let that happen. I offered money to Oscar to keep him quiet. More and more money, year after year.

Over this past month, I began to run out of money. I'm ashamed to say that I started blackmailing people, cheating at bingo, and selling pot at an outrageous price. It was never enough for Oscar. I even offered him my house. Finally, he told me what he really wanted was the diamonds. I refused. I would never give up the ring. It means the world to me. I've now hidden it in a safe place.

As I write this, everything has come to a head. Oscar is furious that Lars has been reelected once again. I believe he is about to release the information about the robbery. I've been trying to reach Beverly to warn her that Lars might be exposed. I want her to be there for him if Oscar goes through with his threats. I know she loves Lars and will protect him to the best of her ability.

Lars swore to me he never told Beverly about the robbery, so it will be a shock to her. He's told me she has a temper that has bordered on violent. She found out at a certain point about our affair, and for obvious reasons, has never liked me. When she hears I encouraged Lars to commit the theft which might be his ruination, it's entirely possible she'll hurt me.

That's everything. You must be severely disappointed in me, and that makes my heart ache. Just know that I loved you as a friend, as a daughter, and as a granddaughter. I am eternally grateful for our friendship. That is the god's honest truth.

I trust you'll do what is right now that I am gone. The diamonds should go to their rightful owner—Fawkes and Sons, which is still in business. Keep any reward money that is offered as I don't have anything else of value to leave you. Please take care of my beloved Sugar. I know she'll bring you the same happiness she has brought me.

One last word: I believe that Jason Banks, who owns Fishes Do Come True down at the wharf, would be a perfect mate for you. I think he has a touch of HSP in him. I was awful to him and I hope you'll apologize for me. I know you're skittish from Adam, but I believe Jason to be of the highest character.

Regretfully, but with all my love,
Trudy

Jason and I stared at each other for several beats. I wasn't even sure where to begin.

I finally said, "If only I'd found this earlier. Stanley could have lived."

Jason put his arm around me. "Please don't blame yourself, Kayla. It's not your fault."

I looked at him helplessly as a big wave of guilt washed over me.

"Do you at least feel better now that you know *why* she turned to cheating and blackmail?" he asked.

"Not really. Couldn't she have gotten the money some other way? And she never told me. I would have helped her if she'd let me know what was going on."

"But . . ."

"What?"

"She knew all of this would upset you. She wanted to be the perfect grandmother in your eyes."

"That's sad, though. That she couldn't trust me to tell me the truth. I would have still loved her."

He drew me closer and kissed the top of my head.

"We have to tell Brian about Oscar," he said. "He needs to be arrested for blackmail."

After I called Brian and brought him up-to-date, I turned to Jason.

"There's a big problem. I have no clue where the ring is."

"Let's sleep on it. Maybe we can come up with something."

He left soon afterward. There was no need for him to stay with me. It was now safe for me to be alone.

THE NEXT NIGHT, JASON CAME OVER WITH PIZZAS. I'd spent the day trying to think of where in the heck the ring could be. I was no closer to knowing. Jason also had come up empty.

He'd brought a veggie pizza for me and sausage and ground beef for himself. The cats liked the smell of his pizza better than mine, so they hopped up next to him on the couch and gave him moony eyes.

He fed them some ground beef and they gobbled it up and asked for more. This went on until I realized Jason hadn't eaten any of his pizza.

"Okay, my loves. Jason gets to eat now." I found their jangly ball and threw it across the floor. They jumped down from the couch to chase after it. The ball made the usual noise as they batted it and pounced on it.

"What's in there?" Jason asked.

"I don't know. Whatever they put in jangly balls. A bell?"

"That's not a bell." Jason, who still hadn't had any dinner, bent to the floor and took the ball away from Sugar, who was none too happy about it. "And there's something strange about the way it rolls. I think it's been broken open and put back together again."

"What are you doing?" I asked as he cracked the ball onto the dining room table.

It fell apart and we gasped. A diamond ring spilled out.

A FEW DAYS LATER AT THE CLUBHOUSE restaurant, Isabella and I debriefed over her kidnapping, the note from Trudy, and the diamond ring. Trudy's attorney, Theodore Patel, had assisted me in getting the diamonds back to the jewelry store, Fawkes and Sons. I received a reward, which I put aside in case my business had a slow period.

"I can't believe I forgot to tell you," Isabella said before taking a sip of coffee.

"Tell me what?"

Isabella looked around the restaurant. "I think Vincent's in the kitchen. I found out why he refuses to order from you."

I leaned forward. "Do tell."

"You'll never guess who makes the desserts he sells."

"Who?"

"He does."

I almost fell out of my chair. "Vincent bakes?"

"Clearly not very well, but yes. He told me it's been his lifelong dream to be a baker. He never gets it right, though. Bottom line, he's jealous of you."

I shook my head in amazement. "That's the reason? All this time?"

Isabella nodded.

"Iz, I can teach him. I'll offer to give him free lessons . . . well, unless you think he'd be insulted."

"Oh, I don't think he'd be offended. It's what he wants to do."

I left for the kitchen. Five minutes later, Vincent and I had scheduled our first baking lesson and he'd placed a major order with me.

JASON CAME OVER AGAIN THE NEXT AFTERNOON. We sat on the couch with Flour and Sugar and ate fish sandwiches he'd brought from the restaurant.

When we finished eating lunch, he said, "So, a new year. A new beginning. The killer and her accomplice as well as the original blackmailer have been apprehended. The diamonds have been returned to the jewelry store. Tristan has started a new painting for you. And you and Vincent have reached a détente."

"All wonderful things," I said.

"You must be feeling pretty good."

"Yes. But I still feel sad about Trudy. And Stanley too."

"I can understand that," he said.

"It's distressing that all these people had secrets. You can't just trust people to be who they appear."

"That's probably true."

Jason seemed distracted as he stroked Flour's back.

"What is it, Jason? I feel like you're not telling me something."

"Kayla, I have a secret. Another one."

My stomach dropped and my heart started pounding. What now? Hadn't enough happened over the past couple of months? I'd had it up to here with surprises, secrets, and change. It was all too much.

"Let's go for a walk and I'll tell you," Jason said.

He led me out the front door, across the driveway, and along the planked walkway. I followed him as he crossed the coastal path and went down to the beach. My throat was so tight I felt as though Lars had strangled me again. I braced myself. Would I be able to get over it? Could I handle what was to come? I walked after Jason all the way to the shore, where he stepped aside and pointed to something written in the sand.

The characters *J.B + K.J.* appeared inside a giant heart.

Jason took both my hands, looked me deep in the eyes, and said softly, "I love you."

THE END

Carol Ayer, a Highly Sensitive Person (HSP), lives halfway between San Francisco and Sacramento with her cat, Rainn. When she's not writing, she's reading mysteries and thrillers or watching movies and cooking shows. As a native Californian, she visits the ocean as often as possible.

9 781603 816298